LITTLE GEMS

JADE

2018

ROMANCE
WRITERS
of Australia

Jade 2018: Little Gems Anthology

Anthology of Short Stories published by Romance Writers of Australia Inc © 2018

Ebook format: 978-0-9872809-6-1

Print format: 978-0-9872809-5-4

Little Gems Coordinator: Lis Hoorweg

Cover design by Lana Pecherczyk

Edited by Laura Greaves

Proofread by Claire Boston

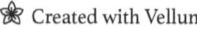 Created with Vellum

OTHER LITTLE GEMS ANTHOLOGIES

Diamond 2012
Sapphire 2013
Moonstone 2014
Peridot 2015
Sunstone 2016
Onyx 2017

LITTLE GEMS

JADE
Short Story Anthology
2018

CONTENTS

FOREWORD

Our central gemstone this year is Jade, and though the most common colour associated with the crystal is green, it actually comes in almost all of the colours of the rainbow. Each of those colours have different mystical properties associated with them, but for writers perhaps the most important are green which encourages creativity, white which filters distractions, and red which dispels fear.

But other colours are associated with emotions that go hand in hand with romance; bringing joy, mirth and happiness, alleviating hurt, and of course love.

The writers in this year's anthology have covered a range of emotions from sadness, despair and grief, to joy, laughter and love. However no matter the emotion, the one thing you can be guaranteed is the stories will have a happy ending.

So without further ado, I hope you enjoy the wonderful stories in Little Gems Jade 2018.

Claire Boston
RWA President 2017-2018

THE JADE KEEPSAKE

ISABELLA HARGREAVES

Old Identities Hotel, Wellington, N.Z., 14 October 1914

My love,

It seems an age since we parted this morning. I promised to write to you every day, and this is the beginning.

I'm holding the beautiful jade amulet you gave me to remember you by. As if I would need anything to remind me of you—the touch of your lips on mine, the sound of your voice rumbling in my ear, the taste of you! Already I long for the day you'll return. No matter what happens, I'll wait for you.

Write to me when you can. Safe journey and swift return.

Yours forever,

Viola

1ST NEW ZEALAND STATIONARY HOSPITAL, Salonika, August 1915

My darling Vi,

Don't worry when you see the address—I'm fine. Managed to get in the way of a sniper's bullet that winged me. My mate, Jimmy from Chandler's farm—you remember him from

Wellington—says I organised it so I'd have more time to write to you because that's all I ever want to do. And he's not wrong about writing to you being my favourite occupation.

I expect to be here for a while then get shipped back to Gallipoli.

I look forward to reading that all is well at home and that those school kids of yours are behaving themselves. Tell them, if they don't, I'll be after them with a switch when I get back.

All my love,

Alec

AHIPARA, N.Z. December 1915

My love,

By now you will be well away from Gallipoli. Thank god!

My class has done very well with their schoolwork this year. So many of the boys are keen to join the Army when they are old enough. I hope they never get the opportunity. It would break my heart to have so many boys risk their lives as you are doing. They are so very young.

I look forward to hearing that you're safe in England before long. Surely they will send you there rather than straight to the front in France.

I miss you terribly and look forward to showing you my new teacher's residence—it's quite unusual for a single woman to be given separate quarters! I've made it cosy, ready for your return, which I hope will be soon.

All my love,

Viola

ENGLAND, March 1916

My darling Vi,

I'm finally in Old Blighty! Never thought I'd make it here until this war started. Almost missed out, thanks to Gallipoli. I've been promoted to sergeant and am doing some training before we're railed out to France. Hope you're proud of me. Can't say I did much to earn it except to stay on my pins.

I wish I could show you London. It would be so much more fun to be seeing the sights with you, rather than with young Jimmy. I've enclosed a souvenir from the Tower for you.

As there are so many soldiers being sent over to France, surely we'll be coming home victorious soon.

All my love,

Alec

AHIPARA, May 1916

My love,

I love the brooch from the Tower and the photograph of you in your sergeant's uniform!

Things go on just the same here. Sometimes the days drag endlessly, despite all my busyness at school. It feels like an age since you were last here and an eternity before you will be here again.

I've coaxed some flowers into growing in the sandy soil and they are putting on a marvellous display. I can't wait for you to see them. My class is behaving pretty well, so I've no reason to grumble.

I long to see you again.

All my love,

Viola

PARIS, France, October 1917

My dearest Vi,

Sorry I haven't written for some time. We've fought our largest battle to date—Passchendaele. So many of the regiment are gone—including Jimmy. It's hard for the survivors to break out of their melancholia. Mercifully, we have leave in Paris for ten days.

I've been promoted again—to lieutenant after officer training school. Can you believe it? Me, an officer! I'll be in England for a few months then back to France with my own platoon.

Hope you're proud.

Love,

Alec

AHIPARA, December 1917

My love,

Of course I'm proud of you! My heart is bursting with it, but also with fear for your safety. When will this war end so you can come home? Please be very careful. I know you—you'll put yourself in danger to save your men for sure. Don't take any risks. I need you home with me.

Mr Lennox collared me the other day and told me there's still a job waiting for you after your return. He said he misses your good humour and reliability. So do I! And so much more.

All my love, Alec.

Viola

FRANCE, August 1918

Dearest Vi,

Everything is hotting up again here. Surely this is the last action I'll see before leave.

I've got a funny feeling about this advance that just won't go away. Never had it before and I don't want it again.

I'm sure I'm just imagining things, but just in case, I want you to know that loving you and imagining coming back to you to build that little cottage we planned has been all that's kept me going these last four years. My will leaves everything I've saved to you and all my possessions here will come back to you. If the worst happens, I want to know that you will make a new life without me, marry and have that family you dream of.

I promise you I'll take care not to go west. But, if it happens, know that I've loved you more than life itself and I'll go on loving you for all eternity. You are my reason for living and my hope for the future.

All my love,
Alec

AHIPARA, September 1918

The sky stretched blue and endless above Viola. Clouds like wisps of belly wool floated over the horizon. The wind off the Tasman Sea plumed the waves and looped loosened strands of her blonde hair across her face and over her shoulders. Golden sand scrunched beneath her feet, sliding between her bare toes.

The straw hat that should have been on her head had long since fled her grasp and flown into the dunes. She would search for it on the return journey.

She escaped here for a few minutes every day. A few minutes to be in the place that reminded her most of Alec and their brief time together before war had separated them and ruptured their bubble of happiness.

If it weren't for the formal studio photographs that he had sent from France, she wouldn't know what he looked like any more. Every time his face blurred in her mind, in desperate fear that she would forget him, she raced to her room to grab his photographs from her top drawer where they nestled amongst her lace handkerchiefs.

The ache of longing in her chest rarely left her. It was only here on the beach that she felt some peace, felt some measure of hope that he would return—one day. Please god it would be soon. She touched the sun-warmed jade around her neck as if she could summon him back to her by doing so.

Never for one minute, when she waved him off from the dock at Wellington, had she thought their parting would be so long; her life put on hold until she knew whether he would come back, whether he would come back whole, or whether when he returned he would even want to be with her still.

He had endured so much in that time, while she had continued on in the same old life, living in limbo.

And when they did meet again, what would they talk of? What would they have in common? She shook her head to scatter her negative thoughts. It would be all right. They would find a way back. She had to believe that.

She turned for home. There was dinner to prepare and school books to mark before she climbed into her lonely bed, ready for the next day to start again.

She approached her little cottage, her wayward hat again in her possession. Through the darkening twilight a blurred figure hurried across her verandah. His sharp rap on her door carried across the gloom.

Viola grasped her skirt and ran. *Alec!*

She puffed up the garden path. At the verandah step, her feet faltered. She halted, bent over, dragging air into her lungs. The figure before her wore a uniform.

But he was too small for Alec. Hope died—plunged like a ballast stone into the pit of her gut. Nausea rose up inside her, threatening to spill her afternoon tea onto her boots.

"Miss Wilks, I have a telegram for you." The post boy held out an envelope. Last year he had been one of her pupils. This year he had an adult's job. "I'm sorry, Miss I ..." His words faded and died. He thrust the paper into her numb hand, motionless at her side, then slipped past her to his bicycle.

Viola sucked in a fractured breath and sank onto the top step. She hooked a finger under the flap of the envelope and tugged the small leaf of paper out.

Regret to inform you Lieutenant Alec Butler missing in action.

The words hit her in the chest like a medicine ball, knocking the air from her lungs. The ink on the sheet in her hand smudged as tears splattered it. She crumpled the words.

Deep chest-racking sobs shuddered out, drowning the nearby waterbirds' roosting chorus. Her heart felt as black as the newly descended night. She clutched the jade talisman around her neck, desperate to feel the familiar warmth it had conveyed since Alec gave it to her.

Now it was stone cold, as though proof he had left this world.

Damp evening air clung to her. She must get inside. She turned to the door, but unable to halt her tears, slumped onto the verandah boards instead. Would the pain ever end?

Slowly, so slowly, her breathing eased, the tears stopped and, unable to find the energy to stand, she crawled towards the door. For long minutes, she leaned against the timber house, her body boneless, her mind blank, her soul riven.

Later, much later, she shivered awake, unbent her stiff legs and pulled herself upright. The door creaked open into the unlit interior. She stumbled inside and found the matches.

Within minutes the flickering flame grew into a warming fire.

Still the jade felt cold beneath her hand.

Viola ghosted through her evening ritual of getting ready for bed without knowing what she did. The children's work-books wouldn't be marked tonight. She didn't care. She didn't care about anything anymore.

AHIPARA, January 1919

Viola scuffed her feet on the damp sand and stared out to sea. Over there to the west was Australia and further west was the vast Indian Ocean, leading on to Europe. It was more than four years since she had watched Alec's ship steam in that direction, taking him away from her forever.

An ache had settled in her heart that she couldn't shift from one day to the next. The world was colourless and she wondered if that would ever change, whether she would ever see the sky as blue again, hear the haunting calls of the ocean birds or feel the soft brush of the sea breeze on her skin.

She trudged back towards the settlement. Marking books awaited. She barely ate now—couldn't get interested in cooking food. She existed as an automaton, no more than that.

She glanced up. A lanky stranger limped towards her from the dunes. His hand shot up and he yelled something in greeting, but he was too far away to be heard. Maybe he was the new teacher replacing her at the start of the school year. She had requested a transfer back to Auckland to be with her family, and it had finally come through. He was a little early, but that would make the transition easier.

Viola waved in acknowledgement and returned to her mindless plodding.

"Don't you recognise me, Viola?" A deep voice cut through the fog of her mind and Viola looked up at the man who had stopped a few feet in front of her. She blinked.

Alec? Was it him?

"Viola, it's Alec," he cried, his words shouted over the background noises of the beach.

"Alec!" How could it be? He was dead. Hadn't she moved on from imagining him everywhere she went? Everywhere they had spent time together.

He spoke again and limped closer until he stood before her, his hand outstretched. "Viola." His voice pleaded.

Her eyes raked his form. Tall enough. His face was different —scarred and with a nose that had been broken and set not quite straight. His hair was streaked with grey. His body so gaunt his clothes hung loosely. Those were Alec's clothes though—from before the war. It was him. She stumbled forward.

He grabbed her waist as she faltered, halting her fall. 'Steady up, old girl." That sounded like the old Alec. He smelled warm and manly like her Alec.

She looked into his dark eyes and saw a world of pain and experience written in them, but also love. Love was still there— after all this time. A sob rose from her chest. She gulped a breath and clutched his shoulders. "You're alive! I thought you were gone forever."

He wrapped her with his arms and dragged her against his chest. "Almost, but they couldn't keep me down," he quipped, his voice rumbling in her ear.

She clung to his ravaged body. Her eyes closed as she savoured the feel of him, the smell of him, the warmth of him for long moments.

She drew back a little and gazed at his face. "Why didn't you write? Why didn't anyone write?"

"No time. I was put onboard on a stretcher, too weak to lift a pen, barely awake five minutes in a day." He gave a grim laugh. "I expect the official notice will arrive eventually."

She thumped his arm with the bottom of her fist. "You can joke about it?"

"Not much choice if I want to stay sane."

She ran her fingers through his dark hair, lifting the waves that had formed since his last military haircut. Sunlight lit the coarse tendrils of silver that peppered the black strands.

His gaze seared hers. "Kiss me, Viola. Make all this seem real."

She nodded once and raised herself up on her tiptoes. His lips met hers with a desperate urgency. She answered him with her own fierce hunger. He pulled her closer, lifting her from the sand. Viola clung to him, never wanting to let him go.

Her lips parted. Their tongues met and danced. Warmth speared through her, igniting her body with four years of longing and unrequited love and lust. Alec was alive, and he was in her arms and she was never letting him go again. She strained to get closer to him. To show him with her body how much she had missed him, how much she loved him still.

The jade necklace heated her neck.

Slowly, inch by inch, Alec lowered her to the ground and eased his mouth from hers. They were both breathless. "Let's go home, Viola. I've so much more love to show you." He looked up at the gathering clouds threatening rain soon. He gave a lopsided grin. "And here isn't the best place to do it."

Viola drew a ragged breath. No, not when there was a cosy bed, a warm fire and privacy at home. She wanted to get there fast. She slid her hand down his arm and threaded her fingers with his, and ran, urging him towards the path through the dunes.

He limped beside her, attempting to keep up. She saw him wince with each step, but push himself onwards.

Everything wasn't the same as in the past. *In the past* he would have scooped her into his arms and run for it. That wasn't possible now.

Instead, Viola stopped, wound her arm around his waist, and leaned her head against his shoulder, then resumed their journey at a slower pace.

Alec was back. For good. They had all the time in the world to share their love. The brass bed in her cosy cottage would be ready, whether they reached it in a hurry, with Alec in pain from his leg injury—or whether they reached it five minutes later, after savouring each other's company along the way, with shared kisses and limbs entwined in mutual support.

Viola raised her hand to the jade, feeling its renewed life and sensing that, now Alec had returned, its life force would give her strength whatever happened in the future.

2

JADED

JANE NEWTON

A sher drained the dregs of the third coffee he'd bought while listening to cheery updates about flight delays. Finally the flight information display board changed to show that QF82 from Singapore had landed. As he made his way to the arrivals gate he scrambled for the sign his assistant had made up for him: SIENNA HASKER. He hoped the piece she was bringing was worth the wait.

Jenna had told him there was an app you could download to check the status of incoming flights, but Asher was old-school and he liked to be punctual. He didn't like using his phone unless he absolutely had to, and he definitely didn't want to be staring at a screen when he was meant to be greeting an important guest on the gallery's behalf.

Holding the sign against his chest, he scanned the passengers making their way towards the bathrooms or baggage claim. None of their eyes lit up on reading his sign.

When he'd almost begun to relax into a slouch, he caught a flash of frizzy red hair above a tired face. When the people around her parted he saw that the small woman was manhandling a large black case he was sure didn't comply with carry-on baggage regulations. She wore a shapeless, faded grey T-shirt. And, dear God, were those clown pants? Bright orange balloon-like things that hid the shape of her legs completely.

Not that he was the slightest bit interested in the shape of her legs.

He raised his gaze to her pale smudge of a face and fixed a smile on his own face. She was definitely heading his way. Not what he was expecting at all. He'd thought Manatee would employ an uptight, bespectacled, grey-suited type to ferry her precious sculpture to the gallery. Maybe he'd have to change the plans he'd made for Sienna Hasker's three-day stint in Sydney. She didn't look like she'd enjoy fine dining, a harbour cruise or the opera at all.

"ASHER STANTON?" Sienna asked and tried to extend a hand to give the gallery curator's a firm shake. But she couldn't put the case down and she couldn't take its weight in one arm, so she changed tack and gave him a firm nod instead. "I'm Sienna Hasker. Lovely to meet you. Manatee is thrilled that the gallery bought her piece. She asked me to extend her deepest gratitude."

Actually Manatee had done nothing of the sort. Instead, she'd barked at Sienna to get her butt on a plane and take the sculpture to Sydney—Sienna's old home—before Christmas. Never mind what personal plans Sienna might have in the lead-up to the holidays. She didn't have any, but she wouldn't tell Manatee that. She never told her anything about herself.

Sienna was under strict instructions to keep the artwork with her at all times until she could hand it over to the gallery curator. Manatee didn't trust international couriers after her amber piece had temporarily gone missing on its way to China.

"Wonderful," Asher said absently as he steered her toward baggage claim. "Let's get your luggage and we'll be on our way."

"Oh, but I'm not staying," she protested. "I'm delivering the artwork to you and turning around for my return flight." She had nothing with her but the sculpture and her handbag. She was certain Manatee said she'd literally be making a flying visit to Sydney to make the delivery, but maybe she should have read the itinerary the gallery had sent her more closely.

She hadn't checked any baggage and didn't intend to stay. She had way too much baggage in Australia already in the form of an ex-boyfriend who'd left her feeling jaded and apathetic about romance.

"Uh, that was the original plan, but my assistant couldn't get you on a return flight straight away. We're putting you up in a hotel for two nights and it will be my pleasure to entertain you while you're here. Didn't Manatee tell you?"

Sienna tried to keep the cringe from showing on her face. "No, Manatee usually forgets little details like that. I really can't stay though. I've got nothing but my toothbrush and a change of underwear in my handbag. I was planning to stay in my travelling pants the whole time." Why had she mentioned her underwear to this man—a professional contact no less? She looked down, hoping he hadn't caught the furious blush creeping up her neck.

"Travelling pants—is that what they are?" He had an odd expression on his face, like he was trying to figure out a puzzle. "Well, I suppose we can stop on the way and I can take you shopping?"

Sienna chuckled. "Sort of like we're Richard Gere and Julia Roberts? That's okay. I think I'll manage."

Now he was turning red, though it wasn't so obvious on someone with such striking olive skin. She inwardly rolled her eyes. She shouldn't be talking about underwear, making *Pretty Woman* jokes or thinking about how nice his skin tone was. He was someone who might buy more of Manatee's work and her job depended on Manatee selling her work. She needed to try harder to make a good impression.

"Then again, I suppose I could use a few things: a nightie, a pair of shorts, a few T-shirts, more underwear." Hmm, it seemed she couldn't stop talking about her underwear.

"Right," he said tightly. "Let's get moving then."

WHILE DRIVING INTO THE CITY, Asher had outlined their itinerary and explained that shorts and T-shirts weren't exactly going to cut it. She'd need a few dresses, maybe some workwear—and yes, a nightie and more underwear. Every time they'd mentioned the word *underwear* he'd pictured her in something black and lacy. Not something he should be doing. She was the representative of an internationally acclaimed artist—not a woman he was trying to pick up in a nightclub.

Not that he often went clubbing to pick up women. He met women at work and at exhibition openings. He dated sometimes, but no one seriously since his ex-fiancée. Putting Lylah firmly to the back of his mind, he led Sienna into a clothing store where he hoped she'd find what she needed for her stay.

He now clutched the weighty carry-on bag. Sienna wouldn't leave it in the car and she'd wanted to get the clothes before they went to the gallery. And she'd asked him to stay close by. So he found himself in the strange situation of waiting outside the change rooms while a complete stranger paraded in and out at regular intervals, asking his opinion on a range of floaty dresses.

He shrugged and made noncommittal sounds, trying not to look too enthusiastic. Without the grey sack shirt and clown pants, he found that he was very interested in Sienna's modest curves and pale but shapely legs. Legs he shouldn't be ogling.

"How is your girlfriend going for sizes?" asked the effusive middle-aged assistant who had helped Sienna select a range of dresses.

"Oh, she's not ..."

"Ta-da!" Sienna stepped from behind the curtain again, this time wearing a figure-hugging pale pink dress.

Asher tried to frown but instead found himself smirking.

"Looks like that's the one, love," said the assistant with a wink at Asher. He tried to shake his head, wanting to explain they'd just met and this was a very short-term business relationship, but the woman barrelled on. "So she's taking that one and the turquoise? And the grey suit? Who's paying for that then?"

He contemplated that a moment. He couldn't ask Sienna to pay when she hadn't expected to be staying—and he had no idea what her financial situation was. But he couldn't exactly put it on the gallery credit card. He could just imagine Miriam from accounting's response when she checked the statement.

"I'll pay for it," he responded. He turned to check Sienna's reaction, but she'd disappeared into the change room again. The assistant led him over to the register and Asher retrieved his credit card. When Sienna asked, he'd tell her it was on the gallery. She didn't need to know.

ASHER HAD LEFT Sienna alone to buy her underwear, toiletries and shoes—which had been a struggle because she'd chosen to hold on to the bag with 'Jaded' inside—but she'd managed somehow, and then she'd quickly checked in to her hotel, showered and changed.

Feeling fresh and crisp in her new grey suit, Sienna cradled the black carry-on bag and followed Asher along the sleek suspended walkway that led to the main gallery. Turning her head from side to side, she hoped she'd have time later to come back and look at the current exhibitions at her leisure.

Asher turned back and she tried not to notice the dynamic line of his classical profile. "Have you been here before?"

She nodded. "Sure, I did a placement here when I was studying art history. I hoped to meet a prince who'd sweep me off my feet and marry me."

He chuckled and turned away. Not many people got her Kate Middleton joke, so she was pleased that she didn't have to explain it to him.

"After we've done the handover and processed the paperwork, the artwork will be placed there." He pointed to a spot in the centre of the room. Obviously they thought it was an important piece. "It'll be part of the permanent exhibition."

She nodded again, determined to stay focused on what they were talking about and not the way his suit jacket lightly caressed his broad shoulders.

"Did you enjoy your placement here? It must have been before my time."

"I did enjoy it—and yes, it was before your time. I would have remembered *you*." Why had she said that, in that flirty tone? She had to keep it together. It was as if she had no control over her impulses. Perhaps she should have had a rest before coming here, but she was looking forward to handing 'Jaded' over so it became the gallery's responsibility.

When they finally reached the office where they processed acquisitions, she placed the heavy bag on a sturdy central bench and unzipped it.

"Extraordinary," Asher breathed after removing the layers of protective packaging and placing the bust gently on a cloth on the bench.

Sienna took a moment to admire the sculpture. This was the reason she'd felt compelled to go to Singapore to work with Manatee, in spite of her well-known 'artistic temperament'.

She'd known the artist's reputation, but she loved her work and the feeling of awe each of her new pieces inspired. The bust of the woman was covered in tiny pieces of jade that were shaped like fish scales. The pieces of jade varied in hue but were identical in size and shape, giving the whole bust an eerie, other-worldly feel.

"Ooh, that's the Manatee piece!" cooed a young woman as she approached them. "She's brilliant—Singapore's Banksy, right?"

Sienna gave a half-smile. Why people gave her boss that name she had no idea. The one-word moniker and a degree of anonymity were the only similarities. And of course if anyone delved a little deeper—i.e. googled her—they would discover several sites giving Manatee's real name and background. It wasn't a huge secret, but Sienna supposed people liked the idea of a mystery. And they liked giving people pithy names that fit neatly into a headline.

"Some people call her that," was all she acknowledged.

"It's not you, is it?" the young woman trilled and then laughed hysterically.

Why was that so funny?

"Sienna studied art history, and she worked at this gallery before she went to Singapore," Asher said. His tone suggested he was defending her: outlining her credentials. Her chest grew warm in response. Before the heat spread up to her neck Asher placed a hand on her elbow and steered her towards the paper-work. "I'll need you to sign the piece over and then Jenna will tie up any loose ends."

Sienna scrawled her signature in the appropriate places and released a long breath, letting go of the tension that had been with her since she'd left Singapore.

"All done. Let's go and have some fun," Asher said in her ear.

Sienna tried to ignore the way her stomach fluttered at that suggestion, and the way Jenna raised her eyebrows at them both.

During the harbour cruise and dinner on Sienna's first night in Sydney, Asher found their conversation had been easy and unguarded. She had told Asher a little about Manatee and her creative process. They'd discovered how much they had in common: she'd studied art history; he had an honours degree in art theory.

They'd both also studied Mandarin. She'd sharpened her language skills while working in and around Singapore, and while travelling in China recently to buy the jade for Manatee's artwork. Asher could also speak Hindi—his mother's native tongue. He'd used his language skills often in his role as curator of Asia–Pacific art at the gallery.

"Are you planning to catch up with family at all during your stay?" he asked during an early dinner in a Japanese restaurant near the Opera House the night before Sienna was due to leave. "Your flight isn't until later tomorrow afternoon, so you have time to see them if you want to. Or will you be coming back again in a few weeks for Christmas?"

Sienna shook her head emphatically. "My parents are both still here—in different parts of Sydney now—but they're busy tomorrow. Mum will come to Singapore to stay with me for a few days at Christmas time; I might see Dad in January." Her tone was light but Asher noticed the glassy sheen to her eyes. He felt compelled to change the subject, to bring the brightness back to her gaze.

"That pink dress is lovely by the way—very... flattering." That was completely the wrong thing to say. It either implied that he'd been busily studying the shape of her body all evening, which he had been, or that there was something wrong with the way she looked and she needed a pretty dress to disguise the problem, which she didn't.

But she shot him a warm smile and sat up a little straighter, running her hands down the sides of the dress. "It's not my usual style, but I do like it."

He knew he should probably draw his eyes away from her and back to his plate, but he found he didn't want to. Sienna coloured a little under his scrutiny but didn't look away. They sat regarding each other until a waiter coughed and asked if it was okay to take their plates. "Sorry," the young man said, looking abashed. "I didn't want to interrupt in case you were going to pop the question or something, but you did say you had a show to get to."

"Oh no, he wasn't ..." Sienna began and then looked back at Asher. But instead of looking upset, she was clearly amused. They struggled to hold in their laughter as they got ready to leave the restaurant.

AFTER THE SHOW, Sienna sat back and let the feeling of satisfaction wash over her. "I've always wanted to see an opera, but somehow I never got around to it." She turned to look at Asher. "Thank you." When his warm gaze met hers, a plummeting sensation hit her stomach. What on earth was going on? As much as she'd tried to keep her distance and steer her thoughts to a professional track, she couldn't quite manage it.

Her mouth went dry as she allowed herself to revel in this new awareness. She was attracted to this man. She liked him as a person. And she wanted to see him again.

AT THE DEPARTURE GATE, Sienna stopped. "I thanked Miriam in

accounting for the clothes but said I'd like to repay the gallery —just asked her to send me a copy of the bill when I got home. She looked at me like I was insane for a second, but then she said that was fine, no need to pay them back."

Asher shifted his weight. "Oh? She can be a bit vague at times."

"You paid for them, didn't you?"

He shrugged and smiled. "Maybe."

"You have to let me know how much so I can repay you."

Shaking his head, he took one of her hands and held it in both of his. "Please don't. There's no need. I couldn't let you run around Sydney in those clown pants for three days."

She laughed and dropped her gaze, but let the subject go for now.

"I have a trip to Singapore coming up in February. Maybe you can do the same for me. I'll arrive in cycling gear and forget my luggage. You can buy me some suits on Orchard Road."

Her eyes met his again. "I'd like that." Warmth flooded through him, and before he realised what he was going to do he leaned forward and pressed his lips to hers. She raised her free hand and delved her fingers into his hair. Her clean, minty scent enveloped him and for a few moments they were lost in the kiss.

Asher finally admitted to himself what several other people had noticed during Sienna's brief stay. This wasn't just a professional relationship and he didn't want to keep his distance. He wanted to stay in touch with her and he couldn't wait to see her again in February—maybe even before that if they could manage it.

He didn't know how they would handle the long-distance thing or exactly what the future held, but he knew he wanted her in it. "See you in February then."

3

SURFING THE JADE OCEAN

JILLIAN JONES

"What on earth is that?" Zoe pointed at the huge jade statue occupying a large portion of Mandy's living room.

Mandy laughed. "That's the reason you're here."

"I don't understand." Had she missed something from their previous conversation? She was visiting Mandy's apartment in Sydney's northern beaches for the first time, to dog- and house-sit for her now ex-boss over the weekend.

"My crazy aunt gave it to me for my birthday because she thought I needed some help in the romance department. The entwined dragon and phoenix is the celestial couple, a symbol of everlasting love." Mandy raised an eyebrow.

"I don't see the connection. Your birthday was six months ago. What does it have to do with you having a romantic weekend away with Pete?"

"I think it has some kind of magic attached to it, because I met him the day after my aunt gave me this. He's The One, and I have a sneaking suspicion he's going to propose this week-end." Mandy jigged up and down, smiling.

In that moment Jackson, Mandy's pug, waddled up,

demanding attention. Mandy lifted him to her chest and snuggled him. "You love Pete too, don't you?" She turned to Zoe. "Come on, touch it. Maybe the statue will magic up the man of your dreams as well." Mandy rubbed the dragon's snout.

She'd never encouraged Zoe to find another man before, and it stirred something deep inside. Zoe hadn't yet voiced the idea of dipping her toe in the dating pond, but the thought had created ripples in the back of her mind over the past few months.

It'd been two years since Nick's death and she'd found herself wondering if it was possible to find love again. How much time should pass before it was okay to invite another man in? Would she even be able to fall for anyone else?

"What if I've already had the man of my dreams?" Zoe replied.

Mandy rolled her eyes. ""Nick would never have expected you to go through life alone."

Maybe she was right. If the situation were reversed, Zoe would want Nick to find love again.

She reached out and caressed the statue. On closer inspection it was beautiful. The coolness of the stone under her fingertips was a soothing balm, enticing her to run her fingers and palm more thoroughly over the smooth green surface.

"You know," Mandy pressed, "a friend of Pete's is back on the dating scene. How about a blind date next Friday night?"

Zoe groaned. "I'm not sure."

"He's twenty-eight, the same as you, and seems like a nice guy. It'll be good for you, but no pressure. He won't be offended if you say no, but I think it's time you got back on the horse." She winked.

"You've already spoken to him about me?"

Mandy nodded, a sheepish look crossing her face.

"Okay." Zoe sighed. Was she ready? Not really, but she was

cornered. She valued Mandy's friendship far too much to say no to her.

ZOE SLID THE CLASP, removing the lead from Jackson's collar, freeing him to go where his heart desired. He immediately skipped over to greet a white poodle. As Zoe stood up, her gaze shifted beyond the fence of the dog park to the beach and landed on three men. Surfboards tucked under their arms, they meandered along the shoreline in animated conversation.

A jolt of awareness struck her.

Zoe couldn't place the other two, but she recognised the longish, dark hair and the distinctive gait of Joshua Nicholls, CEO of the advertising agency where she'd been working for the past three years.

He was tall, with a strong physique, chiseled from the earth. Whenever he walked by her desk at work she sensed his presence as strangely grounding and reassuring. She suspected it was the cologne he wore, because she had no other reason to make that association. He'd always politely acknowledged her around the office, but there'd never been a need for them to interact. She didn't know that much about him, but wanted that to change when he became her boss. Watching him pitch a project to a client was mesmerising, he was a powerful communicator and a creative genius, and she'd soon be under his mentorship. As of Monday she'd be reporting directly to him in her new role as Executive Creative Director.

The men came to a halt, dropped their boards to the sand, and surveyed the ocean. While she hadn't seen his face yet to fully confirm her suspicion, the way he stood when he came to a standstill was further clarification.

In the office, if Joshua stopped to engage with anyone he'd stand exactly like he was now—frozen to the spot as he observed and listened. He looked like a statue. She imagined if he painted himself gold and stood in a busy shopping mall, he'd elicit a few coins from passersby.

However, she'd never visualised him standing on a beach, sans shirt, the effigy of a Greek god. Heat flooded her body as her eyes caressed the undulations of his bare torso. She never would've guessed just how taut and finely sculpted he was under those business shirts.

Her rational mind told her to stop. Ogling her boss wasn't appropriate, but resistance was useless when he defied his usual solidity by flowing in a perfect sun salutation before slipping into some yoga twists. She couldn't help but sigh and surrender in the presence of such strength, form and agility. She was only human.

Retrieving his board, he swivelled around to his buddies, his face in full view displaying ridiculously straight white teeth.

In three years, she'd never seen him flash his teeth in a smile and had assumed he either didn't know how or was self-conscious of his not-so-pearly whites. She couldn't have been more wrong. She made a mental note to recruit him for the next toothpaste ad campaign.

Her voyeuristic capacities took on a whole new level as he paddled out on his board. His arms efficiently sliced the water and the early morning sunlight glistened on the powerful, flexing muscles of his shoulders and back as he effortlessly sailed over several crystal-clear swells.

Slowing down, he swung around to face the beach. Within seconds he was up on his board, riding the crest of a wave twice his height, before sliding gracefully down the front of it. He chased its slow, sensual curve as it folded in on him, crouching and rising, moving back and forth on the board before becoming airborne. Rotating 360° in mid-air, he landed as light as a feather as the water exploded. He emerged, standing triumphantly, as the wave withered to bubbly white and gurgled its way to the shore.

She let out a breath she hadn't realised she was holding. She was seeing him in a whole different light. Her body vibrated with the pure pulsing masculinity in front of her as she feasted on his rippling abs and well-honed chest. The tribal dragon tattoo on his left pec hadn't escaped her attention either. Her gaze travelled up to his face. He was staring at her. His smouldering eyes connected with hers and held her suspended in time and space for a brief moment before he pulled away and turned back to the ocean. She willed her breath and pulse to regulate. She'd been sprung, but she wasn't sure what to make of the weakened muscles in her legs.

Was it the surf calling to her again? She hadn't been on a board in years. Her parents were pro-surfers, so she'd learned to surf practically before she could walk, but she'd tired of their transient lifestyle and rejected it all when she met Nick in her first year out of university. Nick had been everything her parents weren't: he was grounded, reliable and didn't take risks. He had no interest in surfing and he hated the way sand infiltrated everything whenever they visited the beach. She'd put away the part of her that loved the ocean. Nick had seemed so much more important. But two years ago he died in a car accident on his way home from work; hit by a speeding car while the driver had been texting. So why hadn't she moved to the northern beaches and surfed as much as she wanted to after his death? It suddenly hit her. Going back to her old life would be like forgetting him. Disloyal somehow. And she'd lost her confidence.

"THE ARTWORK WILL BE ready first thing Monday," Zoe finished, willing Joshua to look up from the other side of his desk. He'd glanced at her briefly as he waved her into his office, but hadn't shifted his gaze from his laptop in the ten minutes she'd taken to update him.

"Thanks, you've done a terrific job."

She let out a sigh. "Are you surfing again this weekend?" She'd been looking to segue into the topic all week and hadn't found the opportunity. He'd entrusted her with the project, on Monday, her first day in the new role, requesting a progress report on Friday, but he hadn't spoken to her since.

He stopped typing, blinked and looked directly at her for a long moment. His eyes were blue—a beautiful clear ocean blue. She could happily drown in those eyes.

"Maybe," he uttered, breaking the connection when his attention returned to his screen and his fingers continued their movement across the keyboard.

That's it? That's all he was offering? What would it take to have a conversation with him?

"The waves are meant to be as clean as they were last Sunday, pure glass," she pushed.

Again he stopped typing, his pulse becoming visible in his neck, matching her own increased heart rate. Was he angry? She wished she could read minds.

"Did you need anything else?" he asked, not looking up.

Her heart sank as she left the room and the image of surfing the ocean with him fizzled like a spent wave as she made her way back to her desk.

"He hates me." Zoe slumped into her seat and glanced across the desk at Mandy.

"Who?" Mandy lifted her gaze from the screen.

"Joshua. He never looks at me, let alone smiles at me, and he barely speaks to me. I don't think he's happy about my promotion."

Mandy blinked. "He's the reason you got the promotion, the

reason you were hired in the first place, and he fought for you to have three months' leave after Nick's death."

"What?" Had she heard correctly?

"The other directors don't question his authority. He's renowned for his ability to size people up very quickly. Josh was Head of Talent when I first started here."

Questions crisscrossed Zoe's brain. "Do you know much about him?" she blurted.

"His bio is on the website."

"No, I mean his personal life. Is he married? Does he have kids? I've noticed he's never at the social events."

"Oh, you're right, I hadn't realised he'd stopped attending work dos." Mandy's eyes widened. "I wonder why?" She leaned across the desk. "Two months after I started here I asked him on a date because he never had a wife or girlfriend hanging around like the other directors did."

Zoe turned and reached for the glass of water on the other side of the desk to cover her blush. An online search had revealed he was eight years older than her, same age as Mandy, but with no mention of a significant other, Zoe's imagination had run a little wild in the dark and lonely early morning hours of the past three days. And more than once this week, when she'd sensed his presence as he passed her desk, she'd visualised tracing her fingers over his tattoo. She was falling for her boss, which wasn't good. In fact it had the potential to be disastrous.

She took a sip of water and cleared her throat. "What happened?"

"He politely rejected me." Mandy waved her left hand. The blinding sparkle, given off by the diamond rock on her ring finger, was a reminder she was blissfully engaged. "Told me his wife had passed away three months earlier and he wasn't ready to start dating again."

"Oh." Zoe's heart dropped to her feet. No wonder he'd

empathised with her after Nick's death. However, a quick calculation told her his wife had been gone for over four years.

"And has he? You know, started dating again?"

Mandy shrugged and pursed her lips. "Not sure, but I've been unavailable and frankly not interested in him in that way anymore, so I haven't noticed. In any case, give him a chance. You'll find your groove working with him. He's a good boss. He'll challenge you to step up and push the boundaries of any limitation, but he's also supportive." She smiled.

"Okay." Zoe wanted to believe everything would be fine, but she wasn't so sure and her mind was swimming in unanswered questions.

"And speaking of dates, this is Brad's number."

"Who's Brad?"

"Pete's friend. Friday night date. Remember?" Mandy raised her eyebrow as she handed over a yellow Post-It note. "Why not call him now and suggest a drink at the bar across the road?"

Zoe sensed Joshua's presence behind her as she reached for the note. She turned, not missing the fleeting frown directed at her before he dropped a file on Mandy's desk.

"Thanks, it's about time you handed that over," Mandy teased.

"You're welcome." His full, luscious lips curled in a smile. "Have a great weekend."

"You too," Mandy replied as he strode back to his office.

Zoe's heart sank. *He definitely hates me.*

"Anyway," Mandy continued. "Relax and have some fun tonight, okay?"

Zoe nodded, looking hard at the number scrawled on the paper.

"I can't do it." She handed it back. "I'm not ready."

It was still light outside so Zoe hadn't realised the time when Joshua's office door opened and softly closed again, pulling her from the script she'd been writing. Seven o'clock!

"I thought you had a date?"

She swung in her seat to face the human statue, his gaze firmly on her. His eyes like a clean wave she longed to luxuriate in.

"No," she croaked, and swallowed, attempting to repress the butterflies in her belly. "I changed my mind."

"Are you dating again since your husband's passing?"

It seemed he *was* capable of a conversation.

"I'm not sure I'm ready."

"I understand." He nodded and turned, taking two steps towards the lift. He was such a contradiction. So substantial on land yet he defied gravity on the waves. He turned to face her again, catching her staring at him. He blinked and froze. "May I take you to dinner?"

Zoe couldn't believe how effortless it was sharing tapas and a bottle of red wine with Joshua.

They'd eased into the conversation with work chat before turning to surfing, and she complimented him on his impressive surfing skills. He'd been intrigued to discover her parents had been pro-surfers and he encouraged her surfing adventure anecdotes. The conversation flowed to spouses and he'd listened intently to the story of how she'd met her husband before he spoke about his wife and her battle with breast cancer.

"So you haven't been tempted to start dating again?" she asked.

"What do you call this?" He smiled, finishing the last of his wine.

The heat in her chest told her she was blushing. She dropped her head and glanced at the remaining wine in her glass. "I mean ..."

"I'm teasing," he interrupted. "The thing is, I'm not interested in dating just anyone, because there's this woman that caught my eye three years back and well ..." He sucked in a breath. "You know when the ocean turns the colour of jade?"

She nodded.

"Her eyes are that colour, but she was unavailable when I first met her. Now it seems she is, but I'm not sure she's ready to date, or even if she's interested in me."

Zoe's heart dropped.

"Okay." She wasn't sure what else to say. Disappointment sank into her belly. "Who?" He'd been upfront and honest in their conversation so far, she figured he'd say so if he didn't want to share the details.

"You, Zoe."

Her heart stopped.

"My eyes are hazel." It was all she could manage when her brain re-engaged.

"You arrived sixteen months after Jodie's death and sparked an awareness in me. I was drawn to you immediately. Too attracted for my own good." He looked sheepish. "But I could see your skills and talents would be an asset to the agency. I figured, because I was still missing Jodie, the attraction was prompted by loneliness and would abate, but it didn't. It intensified, and keeping my distance was the only way I could hide my feelings for you. Then a year later when your husband passed, I'm ashamed to say I was filled with hope." He held his hands up in surrender as a vice-like grip squeezed her heart and throat. "I'm sorry, it's wrong, I know. But I had to be honest with you." He sighed.

"I had no idea. I thought you hated me," she said when she could find her voice.

"Self-preservation." He smiled weakly, causing her heart to feel it was going to leap from her chest. "I hope knowing this now won't make it difficult for you to work with me."

Zoe grinned. "I think dating will do wonders for our working relationship."

"You're interested?" he choked.

"Yes." She chuckled. "You can't tell?"

"No, but I'm glad to hear it." He flashed that beautiful smile and it melted her. "And you might think your eyes are hazel but take a closer look. There are flecks the colour of a jade ocean." His gaze smouldering, Mandy's statue flitted across her mind's eye.

Maybe it *was* magic.

MY MOTHER'S PENDANT

TONI D'ALIA

One, two, three, four. I matched my steps to the beat of the music playing from my headphones, a jade pendant bouncing on my chest as I ran. Early morning runs along the foreshore boardwalk had become the perfect way to start the day and I relished the sense of calm it brought as I breathed in the fresh salt air from the quiet bay waters.

Beep, beep, beep. The alarm on my phone sounded, marking the halfway point of my run. I pressed the screen on my phone to silence the alarm, took a deep breath, turned and headed back towards my apartment.

I rounded a corner on the path and was mid-step when strong arms grabbed me from behind, dragging me from the track and into the shrubbery. Thrown to the ground, confusion and fear took over as my heart pounded furiously. My breath caught in my throat and I pushed down on my hands, trying to get up. He was on me in one quick move, spinning me around and pushing me onto my back. The jade pendant fell from my neck as he ripped at my clothing. I fought back, punching out at him as anger replaced fear.

Using the heel of my hand, I thrust upwards, catching him on the chin. He fell backwards and I jumped up, desperate to get away, but he reached out and grabbed my ankle, tripping me up as I tried to escape. I fell flat on my stomach, arms out in front. He rolled me around, punching me on the side of my head. My vision blurred, as my head spun from the punch. He straddled me, putting both hands around my throat and squeezing tight.

"Don't move," he whispered cruelly as he tightened his fingers. Keeping one hand around my throat, he moved one hand down, tearing at my clothes.

Adrenaline raced through my system. I bucked furiously, trying to dislodge him. My head ached and my chest burned as I gasped for breath, dizzy and nauseated. Tears escaped and ran down my face as I felt weakness begin to take over.

Then, as suddenly as the attack had begun, it was over and I was free. Drawing in a deep breath, I sat up quickly, scanning the scene. My attacker was sprawled flat on his back, eyes closed and blood running from his lip. Another figure stood over him, fist drawn, ready for combat. With no movement from the attacker, the mystery figure reached down cautiously to check his pulse, then turned and slowly approached me, his hands out in a sign of calm.

"My name is Sam. I'm an off-duty police officer," he said, in a calming voice. "I'm going to call for back up and then we are going to get you all fixed up." Reaching into his pocket, he pulled out his phone and made his call, issuing rapid-fire orders, all the while keeping his eyes firmly fixed on me.

The commotion saw other people join us, muttering and whispering as they took in the scene. Sam was the epitome of calm authority. While talking on the phone, he directed two male runners to secure my attacker until the police arrived.

"It's okay. I'm okay," I repeated to myself.

"You are okay," he whispered once he'd finished his call and had come closer to me.

Tears escaped and a sob broke from my throat as shock set in. My mouth felt dry, my hands clammy. I was going to be sick.

"Look at me. Tell me your name," he asked, gently commanding my attention.

I looked up, finding deep chocolate eyes boring into mine.

"G--Grace."

"Grace, I need you to listen to me. Help is on the way. I need you to lay down," he said. He called to the gathering crowd. "She is going into shock. We need to keep her warm. Throw me your jumpers."

He laid the makeshift blanket over me but I was still trembling. I felt my eyes growing heavy.

"Stay awake, Grace. Focus on me," I heard him say as sirens sounded in the background. Help was on its way.

I WOKE DISORIENTED, the sheets stiff, not at all like the soft cotton on my bed at home. My head throbbed and memories of the attack quickly returned. The aftermath was vivid in my mind as I recalled Sam giving a rundown to the paramedics that had arrived at the scene.

"Her name is Grace. She hasn't lost consciousness. He hit her head hard. She went into shock. Which hospital are you taking her to?"

I remembered being loaded into the ambulance as a young paramedic spoke in a calm, soothing voice, asking for my name and age and noting my injuries. In the background, Sam's agitated voice reported to the officers that had arrived to arrest my attacker.

"Oh, you're awake," said the nurse, interrupting my thoughts as she entered my hospital room. "My name is Nora.

I'm just going to take your blood pressure. How are you feeling? Any pain?" As she spoke, she picked up my wrist, found my pulse and silently counted.

"My head hurts," I said as tears sprung to my eyes.

After taking my pulse, she picked up my chart. "On a scale of one to ten, with ten being the worst, how is the pain?"

"Eleven!" I sobbed. The pounding in my head was intense.

"Okay, well, let me check your blood pressure and then I'll have a chat with the doctor and see what we can do about that," she reassured me.

She wrapped the fabric around my upper arm and fastened it. A machine activated, tightening the cuff as it took my blood pressure. Jotting the measurement on the chart, she returned it to the end of the bedframe. "Just lay back and rest. I'll chat with the doctor about your pain meds."

I laid my head back on the pillow and closed my eyes. The knock at the door a few minutes later startled me and I looked up to see my rescuer standing in the doorway.

"Hi. May I come in?" he asked cautiously.

"S--Sam," I stuttered. "Hi. Yes, of course. Come in."

"I brought these for you," he said, handing me a bunch of flowers. "I would have been here sooner but I had to go to the station to fill out a report. How are you feeling?"

"The flowers are beautiful. Thank you," I got out, then promptly burst into tears.

"Hey, it's okay now, Grace," he said, coming to stand next to the bed.

"I'm sorry. My head is sore and ... "

"Do you want me to get someone to help?"

"No. The nurse just left. She's gone to talk to the doctor." I sniffed as I spoke. "Thank you for saving me today." Tears continued falling down my cheeks.

"Hey, that's okay. I'm just sorry I couldn't get to you any faster," he said, his eyes filled with concern.

I reached out to grab his hand. "You saved me!"

"I did what anyone would have done." He sat on the chair next to my bed. "I wanted to let you know that they've arrested your attacker. He's confessed but you'll still need to make a report. The officers were going to come here, but given that he confessed I persuaded them to wait until you're feeling better."

"Thank you," I said, closing my eyes and putting my hand on my forehead to try and ease the pain pounding inside my head. Remembering the attack, I felt for my necklace. "Do you know if anyone found my necklace? It was a gold chain with a green jade pendant on it. He ripped it off me," I said.

"Not that I know of. Was it special to you?"

"It was my mother's. She always said it was her lucky charm." Fresh tears filled my eyes.

"I'll put in a report at the station."

Nora appeared in the doorway. "I have that pain medication for you, Grace," she said, holding up a clear little cup filled with pills. "The doctor wants to admit you into Short Stays until we have the pain under control." Then, looking at Sam, she said firmly, "Visiting hours are between two o'clock and eight o'clock."

Holding up his hands in surrender, Sam smiled and said, "I'm going. I hope you feel better soon, Grace." Then, bowing his head at Nora and me, he exited the room.

"Oh my, your young fellow is quite handsome," Nora said, handing me the small cup. I downed the pills with a glass of water, laid my head back down on the pillow and whispered, "He isn't mine."

DISCHARGED the following morning with a prescription for strong painkillers and a promise to check in with my family doctor in a couple of days, I took an Uber from the hospital to the police station to make my report. The detective assigned to the case confirmed that my attacker had confessed to the assault, with DNA samples linking him to a further eight assaults on women. He had been sent to the Metropolitan Remand Centre and was awaiting a hearing.

"Now, we understand this is a huge shock to you and it is natural for victims to feel many different emotions after a trauma such as this. As such, we recommend you see a psychologist or counsellor. There is information in here, so please have a read when you are feeling up to it," the detective said, handing me a folder.

We had just finishing when the office door opened. Sam stood in the doorway. His gaze searched me up and down, then rested back on my eyes. "Hey, they released you already." He came to stand next to me. "I've just finished my shift. Would you like a lift home?"

"If it's not too much trouble that would be great."

He walked me to reception and told me to wait while he signed out. He was back by my side in less than two minutes, escorting me to his car.

"So where to, Grace?" he asked.

Giving him my address, he drove me home, helping me to my door.

"Will you be okay? Do you need me to call anyone for you?"

"No. I'll be fine, just a bit tired. I think I'll have a little nap. Thank you for everything." I opened the door and started to walk through when I felt his hand at my elbow.

"Grace, would it be okay if I check on you tomorrow?"

"Yes, of course. I'd like that. And maybe... maybe I could take you to dinner tomorrow night to thank you... I mean, if you're free that is?"

"There's really no need to thank me, but I'd like to go to dinner with you." His face lit up. "Would seven suit you?

"Seven's perfect."

"I'll pick you up at seven then," he said, leaning close as if to kiss me before straightening and pulling away. "Until then."

"Until then," I whispered back, watching him walk away.

A BUZZING SOUND woke me from my nap. Opening my eyes, I stretched, then winced as pain shot through me. I picked up the phone on the bedside table and saw a photo of Beth on the screen as my phone continued vibrating in my hand. Swiping the screen I took the call.

"Hey Chickadee, we still on for tonight?" she asked. Damn, I had completely forgotten I was supposed to be going out with the girls tonight. After a brief run down on the past forty-eight hours, Beth announced she was coming over ... immediately.

LYING ON THE COUCH, I recounted the attack to a horrified Beth. Thoughts of the attack led to thoughts of Sam, my protector. I recalled his strength, his courage, his gentleness. I pictured his deep brown eyes and muscular arms.

"Honey, I need to meet this Sam of yours," exclaimed Beth.

"He isn't mine, Bethy."

"Hmm, really? So where is he taking you tomorrow?"

"He didn't say."

"Well, I want details, missy," Beth said as I laughed at her. "Don't laugh at me, Gracie. The minute you get home, I expect a phone call. Well, that is, unless you are getting b-biz-ee."

"B-biz-ee? Busy? Seriously, Beth. Are we ten?" Laughing, she went to throw a cushion at me I held my hands up in surrender. "Stop making me laugh. It hurts."

Beth quickly became serious again. "Are you okay? Do you need your painkillers? I'm sorry, Grace. I'm an awful friend."

Grabbing her hands, I looked her straight in the eyes and

said, "No. You are the bestest friend ever," recalling our childhood saying.

"Love you long time, Gracie."

"And I, you," I said, closing my eyes as images of Sam
danced in my mind and I thought about our dinner tomorrow.

"Wow, you look beautiful, Grace," he said as I opened the
door the following evening. I had managed to hide most of the
bruises on my face with a decent layer of foundation.

Dinner was at a little Italian restaurant. We sat at the back
next to the fireplace, and talked and laughed for hours.

"Can I interest you in coffee or dessert?" The waiter asked
as the night drew to a close.

"Not for me, thanks," I said, looking at Sam.

"Just the bill, please."

The waiter returned with the little black folder that
contained our bill, placing it in the centre of the table. I went to
pick it up, but Sam's lightning quick reactions saw him reach
it first.

"Please Sam, let me. I would like to buy dinner to thank you
for saving me," I said.

"A gentleman always pays," he said with a smile, silencing
any further discussion.

Once home he walked me to the door, but I didn't want the
evening to end.

"Would you like to come in for a coffee?" I asked.

"I'd love some," he said, holding the door open for me.

I led him to the kitchen and made coffees for us both.

"Thank you for dinner Sam," I said, handing him his coffee
and adding, "I seem to be thanking you a lot." He chuckled as
we sat on the couch in the living room.

"How are you feeling? Are you in any pain?" he asked.

"Only when I move. I have some bruises, but my head feels better. I was lucky you were there."

"I have something for you." He pulled the gold chain with the jade pendant hanging on it from his pocket. "I went back and searched the scene. I found this hidden under some shrubs and had it cleaned and fixed for you."

"Oh, thank you," I said, tears filling my eyes. Sam placed the chain around my neck and fastened the new clasp, the jade pendant falling to sit on my chest. Sam's hand rested on the side of my face.

"It matches your eyes," he said. His finger swept over my bottom lip.

I leaned in and closed the distance between us as our mouths met, soft lips exploring, tasting and discovering. He wrapped his arms around me and passion ignited, his kisses growing more urgent. I winced in pain as he came into contact with my bruises.

"Are you okay?" he asked, concerned, as he broke away.

"Sorry. I'm just a bit sore." I leaned forward gently, my lips meeting his again. Slowly savouring each kiss, no thoughts of time, our kisses grew longer and more intense, until he gently pulled away.

"Grace, I better get going."

"You don't have to go just yet."

"Yeah, I do. You need your rest. But I'd like see you again," he said.

"I'd like that. Thank you for a lovely night," I said as we walked to the door.

"The first of many, I hope," he whispered. His breath caressed my cheek.

"Mm, that sounds nice."

"I'll call you tomorrow."

"Goodnight, Sam," I said, watching him walk away, looking forward to tomorrow when I would see him again, and hoping that there would be many more tomorrows in our future.

A MONTH AFTER THE ATTACK, Sam moved in with me and was by my side at the sentencing hearing for my attacker. The sentence was handed down for all nine attacks, with sentences to be served consecutively, meaning we didn't have to worry about him being free for a long time.

Sam and I ran together every morning on the same path along the foreshore. It was comforting to have someone to run with, the horror of that morning still haunting us both at times. Exactly one year after the attack, Sam stopped suddenly after rounding a corner on the path. It was the site of the attack. I pulled up next to him, putting my hand on his arm to check he was all right.

Grabbing my hands, he turned and looked at me. "Gracie, this is the spot I could have lost you, but it's also the spot I found you." He dropped to one knee and continued, "I love you, Grace, so very much. Will you marry me?"

People had gathered but I barely noticed them as I nodded, tears running down my face. I dropped to my knees to wrap my arms around him. Pulling away slightly, he held out a ring box. Inside sat an exquisite gold band with a translucent jade stone at its centre, surrounded by diamonds.

"To match your mother's pendant, and to keep you safe," he explained, having discovered that many believed that the jade gemstone was a protective stone. I like to think that my mother's jade pendant had protected me the day of the attack, keeping me safe by bringing me Sam; my protector, my love.

5

CUPID'S FAVOUR

NOELLE CLARK

A bbie glanced at her watch. She was early. The meeting wasn't for another half hour.

Chinatown in Brisbane was noisy and chaotic. That's what she loved about visiting the Chinese enclave. Red lanterns celebrating Chinese New Year hung everywhere and the pungent aroma of Asian food made her hungry.

The Year of the Rooster.

Abbie wondered what it would bring her. Good luck? Good Fortune?

She smiled. *Maybe love?*

Abbie was born in the Year of the Rooster, twenty-four years ago. Apparently if you were born in the sign of the New Year you were doubly blessed. You just had to believe.

Colourful stalls down both sides of the mall beckoned. Banners hung from one side to the other. Effigies of the rooster were everywhere. Already crowds were building, browsing through the wares.

"You buy?" A cheap and chunky sparkly bracelet was thrust in her face by a Chinese woman. "Only five dollars."

Abbie shook her head and kept on moving, slowly

browsing the merchant tables. She had no need for any good luck trinkets. She'd already used up all her good luck and look how that had turned out.

When Abbie reached the end of the tables she turned, aiming for the stalls on the other side of the mall. As she did, a solitary, tiny figure caught her eye. At first she thought it was a child in costume. She stared for a moment. It was an old man, so thin his cheekbones shone where his skin perfectly moulded the shape of his face like a skull wrapped in plastic. Wisps of white hair hung from his chin and brushed against his collarbone. On his head he wore a small round black cap.

But it was his eyes that caught Abbie's attention. Pale orbs the colour of milky opal stared out from deep sockets in his skull. Abbie waited for him to blink or move. Anything.

The man sat at a small table not much bigger than a tray, his hands palms down on a black velvet tablecloth that draped almost to the ground. His fingers sported overly long yellow nails. He wore a black tunic, the sleeves covering his arms.

"Come!"

His breathy command, low pitched and forceful, took Abbie by surprise. She took a step back, about to retreat into the crowd and head for the restaurant where she was to meet up with friends for yum cha.

"No! You! Girly! *Come here!*"

His voice, stronger now, sounded so at odds with his frailty.

He tipped his head to one side as though listening, then nodded.

"Good. You're still there. Sit down. I'll tell you something."

Abbie glanced around. The stalls were crowded with people. Surely she would come to no harm. She saw a small stool next to him and sat down.

His mask-like face did not change. She was sure he was blind.

"Good. You are ready."

"Ready? Um, for what?"

Before she could react, he snatched her hand in his repulsive claw. She tried to pull away but his grip was deceptively strong.

"Just breathe slowly. Listen to me." His strong accent made him hard to understand.

Abbie's heart raced. The guy was creepy. But something about his unseeing eyes, macabre in their blindness, was compelling. She took a deep breath and leaned in.

The old man uttered a low monotone hum. She became aware of a tingling sensation where his hand gripped hers, and it felt hot. When he spoke, it was barely a whisper.

"You're better off now without that man called David who loves himself more than he loves you. This year you will enjoy Cupid's favour."

Abbie gasped. *What did he just say? How did he know about David?*

"You are a child of the rooster. You will be doubly blessed." With his other hand he reached into the folds of his tunic and brought out a circular piece of apple-green jade with a hole in the centre, attached to a fine gold chain. "Give me other hand."

Abbie did as she was told, mesmerised by this strange man with the sight of a seer yet blind.

"Chinese call this *yu*. This jade is very special. Hold it tight."

He placed the jade into her palm and folded her fingers over it, then placed his hand over hers and squeezed.

"Now close your eyes."

She obeyed, completely under his spell.

Little pinpricks of light danced behind her closed eyelids then, soon, a foggy cloud shrouded her brain and she succumbed to a peaceful state, her breathing slow and deep.

From somewhere far away she heard voices and some shouting. Part of her dismissed it as just the crowd in the mall celebrating Chinese New Year. But the sounds seemed different. Street noises mingled with the shouting and became louder. Strange odours filled her nostrils. She tried to open her eyes to break the hypnosis or spell or whatever it was the old man had cast on her. She concentrated hard, and finally blinked her eyes open to look around.

A rickshaw pulled by a thin Chinese man wearing only scruffy black calf-length trousers bore down on her. He shouted at her but she didn't understand. Without slowing he headed straight for her. Suddenly she understood and jumped clear just in time to prevent being mowed down.

Her heart raced and she felt herself shaking all over. She reached out to a lamp post and clung to it as she tried to make sense of things. Aware of a tingling sensation in one hand, she saw that her fingers were tightly clenched. She opened them and saw the jade.

She had not the ability, nor the time, to contemplate what was happening. Slipping the jade into her handbag, she concentrated on removing herself from the precarious intersection. Some shopfronts with their wares out on the footpath looked a bit like the market stalls in the Chinatown Mall, but ... somehow different. Everything seemed less colourful. Dirtier, more shabby, and certainly not at all like the place she was used to.

The traffic was chaotic. Rickshaws raced along, the pullers competing with a few old motorcars and trams crammed with passengers.

Totally confused, Abbie took a deep breath and glanced around her. Red lanterns and garlands hung from high above the street. She calmed down. It was still Chinese New Year, of that she was certain. She must have ventured into a part of Brisbane's Chinatown that she didn't know about. She pushed her way through the throng of busy, rushing people. At the corner she turned right, finding herself on a broad promenade. This road was much busier, but less chaotic. Policemen wearing strange uniforms and pith helmets directed the traffic. Derelict looking trucks carrying huge loads jostled in the flow of traffic. The rickshaws kept to the outer edge, looking like a row of ants as they followed each other in a long line.

The road was lined down one side by some lovely buildings with polished granite facades. Abbie walked slowly, reading the nameplates on the buildings. *Hong Kong Shanghai Bank. The North China Daily News. The Shanghai Club.* These were very impressive buildings indeed. She halted when a booming Westminster chime sounded from above. Abbie craned her neck to inspect a clock tower, counting out five resounding tolls. As she did, a young man dressed in a cream linen suit bounded down the wide stairs and collided with her in spectacular form.

Abbie was knocked to the ground. The young man thrust his face close to hers. His brown eyes reflected his concern.

"I'm so sorry! Are you hurt?" He searched her face and then took in her ungainly sprawl on the steps. He grabbed her by one elbow and eased her up to standing position.

"I ... I think so." Abbie was stunned. She didn't know if she was hurt or not. No doubt if she was, the pain would start very soon.

"Your knee. There's blood." He seemed much more distressed about the unfortunate incident than she was. "Look, I was just dashing out. It was my fault. I should have taken more care."

She glanced at her knee and it began to sting. A graze the size of a small saucer oozed blood. Her new summer dress had swathes of grime on it.

The man pulled a fresh handkerchief from his pocket, flicked it open and folded it into a triangle. He knelt down and tied it securely around the graze.

Once finished, he stood, still looking anxious and rather shaken. He ran a hand through his dark hair.

"I'm on my way to my club. It's just around the corner. Come with me and I'll get you patched up properly. And buy you a drink. You look as though you need it."

Feeling suddenly a little light headed, she allowed him to take her by the arm and they walked slowly up the busy thoroughfare, retracing her steps of earlier, and turned into a narrow lane. He stopped at a brass plaque on a red brick wall and pulled a bell rope. A small window in a huge wooden door opened and a wizened Chinese face appeared.

"Good evening, Mr. Gibb." The window closed and the door opened wide.

Abbie hesitated. What was she thinking?

"Look, I don't think ... "

"James. James Gibb. I work for the Chartered Bank. This," he indicated the building outside which they stood, "is a club for the expats that work for a number of banks on the Bund. I can't take you to the Shanghai Club. They don't allow women." He looked at her earnestly. "I promise you, I'm quite respectable."

Abbie thought hard. The Bund? Expats? What on earth was happening? Had she hit her head when she fell?

James released her elbow and brought out his wallet, extracted a business card, and handed it to her.

James Gibb, Esq
Commercial Manager
Chartered Bank
407 The Bund, Shanghai.

∾

"So, James, you are visiting Brisbane? From Shanghai?"

Now it was James's turn to look puzzled. "Good Lord, no. I

noticed your Australian accent, and your—well, rather short dress." His faced flushed when he realised what he had said. "I work here. In Shanghai. I'm from Devon." He took hold of her elbow again. "Come on. A stiff gin and tonic and a clean-up of your knee. Then you'll feel better."

She allowed him to escort her through the door held open by the Chinese man, who wore a smart blue uniform. They crossed an open courtyard and entered a cool, walnut lined salon. James led her to a Chesterfield against a far wall and helped her to sit.

Her knee was really hurting now. Blood had soaked James's handkerchief and dribbled down her shin.

James approached some Chinese men dressed in stylish suits and spoke to them. A few minutes later, a nurse appeared with a black bag.

James indicated the woman in the crisp white tunic. "She doesn't speak English, but she'll clean up your leg. Do you have any other parts that hurt? You can go to a private room if you prefer."

A waiter brought over a tray with a long gin and tonic and what looked to be neat whiskey in a tumbler, no doubt for James.

"Here is fine." Abbie began to feel a little better now that she was sitting down. "Thank you."

James took her G and T from the tray and passed it to her, and the nurse began to wash the wound with disinfectant. Abbie sipped on the drink and considered her situation.

"Are you telling me that I am in Shanghai? China? How can that possibly be?"

James pulled up a chair and sat. "Look—er, what is your name, by the way?"

"Abbie Anderson."

"Abbie. I like that. Well, I don't know how you came here,

by ship I suppose. Perhaps I should call for a doctor to examine you. You seem to be ... all of a muddle."

Abbie glanced at her watch but the glass had cracked and the hands were motionless. She must have smashed it in the fall. She wondered if her friends were waiting for her at the Golden King restaurant in Chinatown, where they were supposed to meet. She glanced at the festoons of red lanterns and other decorations cascading lavishly from the ornate plaster ceiling.

Abbie indicated with her hand. "These decorations. Is it Chinese New Year?"

James smiled, as though pleased that this odd girl had finally said something he understood.

"Well, yes. Spring Festival. It's the Year of the Rooster. That's my zodiac year, so I'll be doubly blessed with good fortune, happiness, and good health. That's why I was rushing and sadly crashed into you. I'd just finished work but had to drop some paperwork off at the Customs House. I'm due to meet up with some friends here for dinner and then we're heading out for the celebrations."

The old man. The jade.

Abbie reached into her bag and took out the jade.

"That's pretty. Let me put it on for you." James reached around and clasped it.

"There." His warm smile, genuine and endearing, lit up his handsome face.

Abbie put a hand to her throat and fondled the pendant. She closed her fingers around it and shut her eyes. Her fingers began to tingle, just like they had when the old man had handed the jade to her.

"Tell me, James. What year is it?"

He pulled a funny face. "It's 1921. Why on earth do you ask?"

Abbie took a large sip of her G and T. Then another. The

nurse took Abbie's wrist and checked her pulse, then spoke to James in Chinese.

"You're all patched up now. The nurse says you should rest. No walking or dancing this evening." He looked relieved, yet disappointed at the same time. "I am truly sorry for being the cause of your injury. I do hope that you will allow me to make it up to you when you're feeling better. Perhaps you will have dinner with—"

Rapid gunfire, close by, caused Abbie to jump to her feet. Her first thought was terrorists and she was ready to run and take cover. The gunfire continued, and the smell of gunpowder filled her nostrils as the air became smoky. Then, loud crashes, as though a battle was taking place, jolted her senses.

"Quick! We must run!" She tugged at James's sleeve. "Now!"

Two strong arms encircled her, holding her tightly. He leaned forward, his face only inches from hers, his gaze penetrating.

"Don't be alarmed!" He spoke loudly so as to be heard over the din. "It's the firecrackers. The Lion Dance has begun!"

Abbie turned as a huge, menacing lion head with big beady eyes, a mirror stuck on its forehead to ward off evil, and a single horn protruding from the top, lurched in through the main door and across the lobby of the club. The body of the lion writhed in time with clashing cymbals and beating drums. It was both terrifying and fascinating at the same time.

The lion paused in its writhing to stare at her for a few seconds. The cymbals stopped. Then a shrill scream emanated from the lion and it began dancing again. The cymbals and drums started up, too. The lion headed straight for Abbie. It came close, rhythmically swaying to and fro. Another ribbon of red fire crackers burst into staccato fire. The lion nodded its cumbersome head at her, then turned away and continued on its dance down the corridor.

"Abbie! Abbie!" She searched the crowd for James. "Abbie!"

She tried to see who was calling her. The acrid smoke from the firecrackers hung low, the stench strong and the cymbals deafening.

"There you are! We thought you weren't coming."

Abbie stared into the face of her friend Sophie. *Where was James? What was going on?*

The Lion Dancers moved further on, the din from the drums and cymbals now less raucous.

"Oh my goodness, what have you done to yourself?" Sophie, mouth agape, scanned Abbie from head to foot. "And you've hurt your knee! What happened? Is that why you're late?"

Without waiting for a reply, Sophie grabbed Abbie by the hand and towed her away from the crowded mall.

"We've already got a table. Come on, I'm starving."

Sophie led Abbie into a noisy, garishly decorated restaurant. Trolleys of yum cha clogged up the aisles between tables. The large room resounded with echo from the crowds there to enjoy the Chinese delicacies.

"We'll hit the bathroom first. Got to clean you up. You look awful."

Sophie wet some paper towel and dabbed at the dirt on Abbie's dress while Abbie did her best with her hair.

"Hey! Love your jade." Sophie leaned closer to inspect the jade hanging around Abbie's neck. "Is it new?"

Without waiting for a reply, Sophie ran her eyes over Abbie. "You'll do. There's someone I want you to meet. A friend of mine from England. He works for a bank."

Sophie again took Abbie by the hand and they wove their way to the table, where several other people waited. They looked up from their conversation as the girls approached.

"Abbie, I want you to meet James," Sophie gushed.

A young man with warm brown eyes and dark hair stood and extended his hand.

"I'm very pleased to meet you, Abbie." His eyes flickered momentarily to the jade around her neck.

His English accent ...

Abbie took his hand. His grip firmed as he stared into her eyes.

She smiled. "Tell me, James. What Chinese zodiac year are you?"

He cocked his head to one side. "Rooster. I'm supposed to be doubly blessed this year." He smiled at her. "And you?"

6

THE JADE HEART

PHILLIPA NEFRI CLARK

"It is the colour of your eyes, Izzie."

"I know, Mum. We talked about this earlier, do you remember?" Isobel Davis tucked a stray hair behind her mother's ear with a smile. "I'm going to buy the Jade Heart back today and then you can wear it whenever you wish. All day, every day."

"Tell your dad. He'll be so happy you found my pendant!"

Isobel grimaced. He was the reason it left the family in the first place, pawned to pay off gambling debts more than twenty years ago. Along with just about everything else not nailed down. Well, he was long gone, and at last her mother's beloved heirloom was within reach.

"Are you going to get it now?"

"Hm? Oh, not just yet, Mum. The auction is later today. See here?" Isobel passed a folded newspaper to her mother and pointed to the circled pendant. "Starts at two this afternoon, so I've got time to read to you."

"And Terrance?"

"And Terrance."

"Hurry up. Let's go." Margaret Davis shook the newspaper and Isobel laughed.

"Is he out under the oak tree? I bet he is." Isobel pushed Margaret's wheelchair through the open doors of Forest View Residential Care.

Five years ago, a terrible car accident robbed Margaret of her mobility and damaged her memory. Here she had the best of care, worth every cent Isobel paid.

When Isobel saw the Jade Heart advertised in the auction, she'd had next to no savings. Didn't matter, she rarely played her old Maton guitar. Three phone calls and she'd found a buyer.

"Ter-rance!" Margaret called, waving the newspaper at an older man on a bench. She didn't notice his lack of response.

Isobel almost turned the wheelchair around when she saw he had company. Expensive suit jacket tossed over the arm of the bench, the dark-haired man beside Terrance was an unwelcome sight.

She knew him all too well, and not at all. Her small flat overlooked a casino and he regularly stepped out of his Maserati with some gorgeous woman on his arm. Bartholomew Brown, heir apparent to the fortune of his uncle. Playboy. Adventurer. And hot.

Isobel leaned down to whisper. "Let's come back later."

"No, Izzie. Terrance, you don't mind us sitting with you?" Margaret beamed at Terrance and waved at his visitor, the newspaper flying out of her hands.

Bartholomew Brown got to it just before Isobel, scooping it off the grass in one fluid motion and holding it out with a smile. He was taller than Isobel expected. And he looked after himself, with those powerful shoulders testament to weight training. Or some other muscle building activity. *Stop it!* Isobel dragged her eyes to his face.

Bad idea. Warm brown eyes regarded her with obvious humour.

She cleared her throat. "Um, thanks."

"Shall I return it to your mother?"

Isobel realised he still held the paper out. She curled her fingers around the furthest edge from his hand. "I'll take it."

"I'm Bart."

"I know."

"The normal response is, 'And I'm Izzie'."

"How do you know my name?"

"You mother called you Izzie just then."

"Isobel, actually. May I have the paper please?" She pulled a little and he let go.

Bart nodded toward Margaret, who'd manoeuvred her wheelchair beside the bench and was involved in an intense one-way conversation. "She cheers him up."

"She loves talking to him, even if he can't answer. But I think he does, in his own way." Isobel watched Terrance blink faster as Margaret laughed at her own joke.

"The stroke left him a shell of his former self." Bart spoke quietly. "You read to him, don't you?"

"Mum forgets stuff since her accident, so I read her the old books she once loved. I think he likes them, too." Isobel's face lit up.

Bart leaned a little closer and the heady scent of sandalwood with a hint of lime filled Isobel's senses. "Thank you."

"For reading to them? It's a little thing."

All too aware of Bart's eyes on her, Isobel hurried to Margaret. She dropped onto the bench between her mother's wheelchair and Terrance. "Now, what shall we read today?"

ISOBEL GAZED at the Jade Heart. Her childhood memories didn't do it justice, and with a jolt of disappointment, the three thousand dollars in her purse felt like three dollars.

On a fine gold chain, the emerald-green jade pendant was cut into a love-heart. Twelve small diamonds set in gold formed a frame, sparkling under the lights in the auction room. She knew her great-grandparents' initials were carved into the back from their own wedding, before it became an heirloom, worn by bride after bride. *Until Dad ruined it.*

Isobel turned away to find a seat at the back. An elegant, highly perfumed woman brushed past. She stopped at the Jade Heart.

Afraid this might be competition, Isobel sank onto a chair, fingers interlaced. She exhaled when the woman moved away.

"Sounded like a sigh of relief."

Isobel's gaze shot to Bart's as he sat beside her. "What are you doing here?"

"I like auctions. Never know what one will find. And you left this behind." He handed her the newspaper, still folded to show the circled Jade Heart. "Thought you might need it."

"You followed me here?"

Bart frowned. "You're welcome."

The words hung between them. Isobel looked away, biting her lip. *What's wrong with you?*

"It's a pretty pendant. Are you going to buy it?"

She glanced back at him. "I hope to."

"I'm not a stalker, Izzie." He grinned suddenly, and with a life of its own Isobel's heart flip-flopped.

"Five minutes. Please take your seats." The announcement from the auctioneer reminded Isobel why she was here. Not to buy a 'pretty pendant', but to retrieve an heirloom squandered by a gambler.

"You might not be a stalker, Mr Brown, but I know what kind of man you are." The words tumbled out with no filter, delivered in a monotone, her body language stiff.

The warmth left his eyes. "I very much doubt it, Izzie."

"Only Mum calls me Izzie." Heart pounding, she kept her face expressionless, willing him to get the hint.

With a small shake of his head, Bart got to his feet, hesitating as though wanting to speak. But he walked away and Isobel slumped in her seat and closed her eyes.

AT FIRST, Isobel was confident. Her initial bid lingered long enough for her to believe it was hers, but then someone else chimed in, and bit by bit the price increased.

At two thousand dollars, the other bidders dropped off and Isobel willed the auctioneer to hurry through his *once, twice, three times, sold*. But at 'twice' the perfumed woman raised a finger.

Isobel bid back and forth in small increments, barely able to breathe as her limit got closer, until the other woman turned a glare upon her and bid five thousand dollars.

The auctioneer looked at Isobel, who sat stunned. It was over. That kind of money was outside her reach, and now she'd let her mother down.

Tears stung her eyes and she slipped from her seat to escape. At the door, a small moan caught in her throat as the auctioneer called for last bids, dragging it out. She pulled rather than pushed the door.

"Here, let me."

Why was he still here? The tears spilled over as Isobel glanced at Bart's face through wide eyes. He held the door open and somehow she managed to walk, not run, through it.

IT TOOK HALF an hour and a box of tissues before Isobel

stopped crying and managed to drive home. Somewhere between sobs and sniffles, she'd seen Bart exit the auction house. He'd stood on the edge of the pavement, looking one way and then the other. To imagine he searched for her was preposterous.

Besides how rude she'd been to him, why on earth would a man of his wealth and station be interested in an office cleaner, who lived in jeans and rarely applied makeup?

A long shower didn't really help. Tomorrow she'd visit her mum and break the news. The Jade Heart belonged to someone else, and probably always would.

She threw her phone and keys into her handbag in the kitchen, then glanced at the guitar rack on the wall in the living room. Empty. Her beloved guitar gone now, and just as well. It was time to stop dreaming and get on with the life she had. And go to work.

THE MORNING WAS as grey and drizzly as Isobel's thoughts when she parked at Forest View. No sign of the Maserati, thank goodness. *Please be in your room, Mum. Away from prying eyes.* She visualised the disappointment on her mother's sweet face.

She wasn't in her room. Or in the common room. Isobel followed the sound of Margaret's voice to a small covered patio.

"And my mother handed it to me on the very day of my wedding. Oh, how beautiful the Jade Heart made me feel, and one day my own daughter will wear it when she marries."

Margaret sat with several other women, who were all listening to her speak. How could Isobel tell her now? The silly tears welled up again and she stepped back from the doorway. Then her mother turned her head and Isobel's hand flew over her mouth.

The Jade Heart hung from Margaret's neck.

"Darling! Come and see." Margaret held her hand out, and somehow Isobel found herself perching on the arm of the closest chair. "You clever girl." She grasped Isobel's hand.

"Mum, I ... "

"It's okay. I knew you must have been at work when you didn't come back yesterday, and when that lovely man arrived with it I was so excited. Oh dear. I forget his name, but he knows Terrance."

"Bartholomew Brown?"

"Bart! Yes, that's who. He slipped the box on my lap and said to tell you 'thank you'."

"Thank you? Bartholomew Brown gave you this?"

"No. You did. But he brought it to me. I was telling everyone you'll wear it one day, too. Just like I did marrying your wonderful father."

She kept chatting but Isobel barely heard her. *Why?* What motive did Bart have? Her stomach churned. Now she'd have to distress her mother by giving it back to him. But not yet. Not today.

"Izzie, darling? Are you feeling all right?"

"Mum, I'm ... I have to go. But I'll drop in tomorrow." Isobel kissed Margaret's cheek and rushed out of the room.

Straight into the rock hard chest of a tall man in jeans and t-shirt. One who smelt of sandalwood with a hint of lime, a chuckle deep in his throat as he steadied her with firm hands.

Even as her mouth formed 'excuse me', her brain registered who he was. She pushed herself away from Bart, eyes blazing. "How could you?"

The smile dropped from his mouth. "The pendant?"

"You had no right."

Isobel spun around and stalked off.

Slow, heavy raindrops fell as she reached the car, outrage blinding her to the storm clouds above. Next to her little old Fiesta was Bart's sleek sports car. Such a stark comparison of how far apart they were. His lofty world and her day-to-day struggle. Nothing in common except those few moments yesterday. Which she'd probably imagined anyway. How could she feel a connection to a stranger in such a short time?

"Izzie, wait!"

Leave me alone! Isobel couldn't get her car keys out as her hands were shaking too much to unzip the pocket in her handbag. Bart loomed in her peripheral vision and she turned away.

"Okay, what is going on?"

She ignored him, still trying to get her keys.

"You're getting drenched. Come sit in my car and I'll help you find the keys, assuming they're what you're looking for and not a fork to stab me with?" His tone was mild and she glanced at him.

"No." Her fingers co-operated and she grabbed her keys.

"You're angry."

"I'll let Mum enjoy the Jade Heart for today and return it to you tomorrow." Isobel unlocked her car and opened the door.

"Don't be ridiculous. Nobody cries at an auction unless they've just lost something of great meaning."

Isobel tossed her handbag into the car and put one foot in. "The whole reason Mum lost her family heirloom was because of a man who couldn't pay his gambling debts and I won't allow another gambler to return it. I just won't!"

"Another gambler? Do you mean me?"

For a second, as confusion clouded Bart's face, Isobel wondered if she'd made a terrible mistake. Then she remembered the joy in her mother's eyes. Tears of sheer frustration flooded her eyes as she threw herself into the car and started the motor.

Hair plastered to his head, Bart stood immobile as she backed out, his expression stony.

BY THE TIME Isobel parked and ran to her building, she was soaking wet. Rain came down in sheets and thunder boomed overhead.

She no longer knew the difference between rain and tears, barely able to see in front of her as she stumbled through the entrance. All she longed for was the solace of her flat and a pillow to weep into.

Halfway up the first flight of stairs she lost her footing, sliding back to the bottom with a cry. A few stunned moments later, Isobel prodded herself for damage. No bleeding and nothing broken, thank goodness. She couldn't afford to miss work. But when she tried to stand, her ankle gave way and she almost fell again.

Strong arms came from nowhere to sweep her up like a baby. "I've got you." Bart held her firmly against his chest, his eyes boring into hers. "Don't bother arguing. Where's your flat?"

Something about his tone of voice filled Isobel with over-whelming relief. "Two floors up."

He carried her all the way to her door without another word, setting her down gently to let her find the door key. She swung the door open and he immediately picked her up again.

Inside, he sat her on the sofa and went back to close the door. There, he stopped, his eyes serious. "I'll go once I know you can walk. And are in dry clothes. But your mother shouldn't suffer because you hate me."

"I don't hate you."

He glanced around and Isobel cringed. Her tiny flat was

tidy but so old and worn he must think she had no future. No talent.

"Stop judging me, Izzie. Is that what you sold to pay for the pendant?" Bart pointed at the empty guitar rack.

"What makes you think I sold anything?"

"Your mother remembers more than you think. Like your dream of being a performer. She doesn't understand why you're not."

"Lack of talent."

Bart raised an eyebrow and Isobel's heart fluttered.

"Lack of money, I think," he said. "Forest View is expensive."

"Look, the point is I'll give you back the Jade Heart once I explain to Mum—"

"Is it because of that?" Bart strode to the window and gestured across the road. "The casino?"

"I hate gambling."

"Because of your father. But I'm not him, Izzie."

"But you own a place he'd have gone to." She couldn't keep the bitterness from her voice. "Where problem gamblers go."

"No, I don't." He crossed back to the sofa and sat carefully so as not to touch Isobel. "Let me ask you something random. Do you like Terrance?"

"What? Well, yes. I don't really know him, but Mum does."

"He is my uncle. Terry Brown, owner of the casino and a dozen other properties, including Forest View. I'm in the process of selling everything except the place he now calls home, as your mother does."

Isobel stared at the carpet. Maybe just once she'd learn to ask questions first. Why this gorgeous man was still in her flat was beyond her. "Why buy the pendant? I'm a complete stranger."

"A stranger who reads to a man who hasn't spoken in two years. Please look at me."

She forced herself to meet his eyes. They drew her into his soul and for the first time in her life, Isobel was safe. Warmth rushed through her when he took her hands in his.

"After you left yesterday, before I brought you the newspaper, Terry spoke."

"Oh my goodness! What did he say?"

"Izzie. He said, 'Izzie'. In spite of being a little fireball where I'm concerned, you've made a difference to my only relative. So stepping in to retrieve a family heirloom seemed a nice way to say thank you."

"Oh."

"Oh, indeed."

There had to be a reason this wouldn't work. "What about those gorgeous women you take to the casino?"

"You've been watching me, Isobel Davis! What about them?"

Careful of her ankle, he lifted her onto his lap. She giggled when droplets of rain dripped from his hair onto her face and wiggled until he held her too tightly to move.

"I didn't buy them a family heirloom. Nor do I carry them up two flights of stairs. Just accept it, Izzie."

"Accept what?"

"The Jade Heart. It does match your eyes."

Bart lowered his head, stopping a breath away from Isobel's mouth. "And one day it will look perfect at your wedding."

Eyes wide, she had no chance to answer as he captured her lips with his.

7

TAKE THE CAKE

SHAYNE COLLIER

"Second?" Cate's gasp caused heads to turn in the Country Women's Association hall.

Someone must have made a mistake. This couldn't be happening. "*Second?*"

As if asking the question twice would change anything.

An array of cakes and slices weighed down trestle tables covered in crisp white tablecloths.

Chocolate cakes were spread out at the far end, and next to them Madeira cakes, then a selection of banana loaves, vanilla and caramel slices, lamingtons and sponges.

Cate's attention remained glued to the display of eight Queen Victoria sponges. Even though the competition rules stipulated a standardised recipe, Cate's entry stood out from the rest.

Her feather-light sponge looked like it might float to the ceiling if not for the red ribbon that weighed it down.

A slice of cake had been removed by the judges so it was evident that Cate's bottom and top sponges were both the same size, separated by a delicate smear of home-made strawberry jam topped by a thicker layer of whipped cream. As a finishing touch, she'd adorned the golden top with a dusting of icing sugar and artfully arranged a wreath of strawberry slivers.

"A red ribbon. This can't be right."

"Mum." Emma squeezed Cate's hand with some urgency. "Second is nothing to be ashamed of. Second is good. It's not third. No one ever remembers third."

Cate tried her hardest to hold back the tears.

She had expected to win. The cat was in the bag or whatever that saying was.

But now she had to deal with second.

How could she front up to work at the tractor dealership on Monday or walk down the street without people pointing and muttering, "Poor Cate. Thank goodness her mother and grandmother aren't alive to see this."

She squinted at the entry with a royal blue ribbon across it that featured the gold embossed *FIRST PRIZE—WEBELONG VALLEY SHOW 2018*.

"What's so special about this? It's so lacking in ... " Cate faltered. There were no words to describe this heavy-handed effort.

"Finesse?" Emma offered.

Cate snapped her fingers. "Exactly. Finesse. Style. Elegance."

She screwed up her nose as she bent over the winning entry.

Everything about the cake looked wrong. The wonky bottom sponge didn't match its thinner partner and the decadent pile of cream slapped between the two looked like it had been whipped into submission.

As for the jam, you needed a magnifying glass to see it.

The top of the cake screamed total overkill, piled high with halved strawberries and doused in icing sugar of snowdrift proportions.

She sniffed with exaggerated disdain at a vaguely familiar

aroma and quelled the wild leap of joy from her taste buds, tempted by the summery freshness of sweet strawberries balanced by fragrant bitter orange.

Emma took a step back to examine the offending concoction. With eyes narrowed and arms crossed she inspected both cakes, occasionally uttering "mmm" and "ah".

After what seemed like an eternity, Cate couldn't take it anymore. "Well?"

Emma edged closer to her with a furrowed brow, reminding Cate of a wary child about to pat an unfamiliar dog.

"I don't know, it does smell sort of nice, sort of tasty, maybe even ... yummy." She paused and tentatively touched Cate's arm, a diplomatic gesture. "But your sponge—*your* sponge could grace the cover of any foodie magazine. It's perfect."

Cate pressed her lips together to stop them trembling. What did she expect from her 18-year-old daughter? A lie to heal her bruised ego?

"Em, this isn't fair on you, asking you to choose which cake is the best just to protect my thin skin. Mine looks great but looks aren't everything."

She reached her arm across Emma's shoulders and pulled her close. "Remember what I always told you when you were growing up: it's what's on the inside that counts. This winning entry must taste delicious."

Impishly, she added, "In a French-provincial-meets-earthy-peasant-food sort of way."

"If you're interested, I can share my secret recipe."

Yikes. Cate spun around like a schoolgirl who'd been caught smoking behind the toilet block.

"Oh ... gosh ... is this yours?" Nervous laughter as she peered intently at the card propped against the cake that read *Entrant #7: Gus Fiorelli.*

"My daughter and I were admiring your sponge. It looks so ..."

Gus cleared his throat. "French provincial, maybe? Or what about earthy peasant food?"

Heat flared in Cate's cheeks and she sensed Emma beside her, her lithe body rigid with embarrassment.

He extended a hand. "You must be Cate Sutcliffe. I'm Gus Fiorelli."

Cate made sure her hold was firm but brief. She would ignore the pleasant tingle in her hand after she pulled away.

And no way would she ask him how he knew her name. That was obvious enough. She stood out as the envious second-place getter.

"Nice to meet you. This is my daughter, Emma."

Gus shook Emma's hand. "You must be *the* Emma Sutcliffe. I saw your blue-ribbon banana loaf. Sensational icing. Moist cake with a caramelised sheen."

As Emma brushed away strands of her auburn hair from her pale skin, Cate noticed an almost imperceptible change in her height, as though she had pulled back her shoulders and raised her head to reveal one of her rare smiles.

Emma laughed self-consciously and Cate nearly reeled from shock. Anyone who could get a positive reaction from her shy daughter deserved a medal.

"That was the goal, to create more than your run-of-the-mill banana loaf," Emma said.

"Well, you've done that. Have you ever thought about going commercial?"

Cate read her daughter's sharp intake of breath and interjected in helicopter-parent mode. "That's something to possibly consider down the track."

Over Gus Fiorelli's shoulder, she recognised one of the CWA members making a beeline their way. Best to escape before Charlotte van der Kamp, queen of the vanilla-slice class for three consecutive years, swooped like a falcon on a pair of hapless rabbits.

"It was great to meet you, Gus, but we have to get going."

She ignored Emma's nudge in the ribs.

Charlotte had been distracted by a horde of CWA elders, as Emma liked to call them, so there was still time to exit via the kitchen at the back of the hall.

Emma linked her arm in Cate's. "Mum, I've got an idea. I think we should take Gus up on his offer. If he shows us his recipe ... "

"You'll show me yours," Gus finished.

Emma and Gus chuckled.

"Mum, let's make a date with Gus, have him over for tea."

Cate wondered what had inspired Emma's enthusiasm. It would be like dining with the enemy.

She managed a feeble smile and non-committal, "Okay."

Too late. Charlotte van der Kamp arrived and moved in close—too close, Cate thought—to Gus.

"Cate, Em, so wonderful to see you. You've already met our new shining star, our first non-female entrant, and winner, since the organising committee made the ruling to allow male competitors," Charlotte gushed as she clutched at Gus's shirt-clad arm with the animated fervour of a fan stalking a celebrity.

Cate was blinded by the whiteness of Charlotte's teeth, the neon-red lips, sheen of thickly applied foundation, and false eyelashes that seemed to flicker as fast as the wings of a hummingbird.

"Gus moved here from the big smoke a couple of weeks ago," Charlotte continued in an overly loud voice, "and he's already put up his hand to bake several trays of scones for our next market day."

Was there nothing this man couldn't do? In a matter of minutes, he'd won over Emma. And charmed the granny knickers off the local CWA members, figuratively speaking.

Cate smiled at the thought of a row of grandmas' undies fluttering in the breeze.

For the first time, she paid attention to Gus's appearance and did a quick scan—tall, maybe 6'2", full head of dark hair streaked through with grey, clean-shaven with good skin for a middle-aged man, slim but not scrawny or brawny, and nice eyes and lips. Eyes possibly blue but she couldn't tell without her glasses.

"Congratulations. The biggest achievement for any newbie in this town is to get the CWA on side," she said, keeping the resentment at bay.

Gus grinned right at her. *Nice teeth*, she thought distractedly.

"I don't know about that," he said. "I think I still have a few people to convince."

Charlotte batted her eyelashes at Cate and Gus, looking like a confused Cavoodle.

"I'm not sure if you know this about Cate's family, Gus, but they have a long and honourable association with the CWA," she said. "Cate's mother and grandmother were unbeatable in the Queen Victoria sponge class. I can't recall another winner's name on that hallowed trophy."

In that instant, the atmosphere in the hall became unbearably oppressive. The walls seemed to warp inwards, the cathedral ceiling sagged and Charlotte's features slid down her face towards her ample freckled cleavage.

"If you'll excuse us, we were just leaving." It was Emma, timid Emma, sounding polite yet forceful and in control.

Cate let Emma slip a hand under her elbow to usher her away from the crowd and into the fresh air and afternoon autumn sunshine.

It wasn't until she hopped into the passenger seat of the car and handed the keys to Emma that Cate started to cry.

FOR AS LONG as Cate could remember, the Queen Victoria sponge trophy occupied pride of place on the mantelpiece above the fireplace in the Sutcliffe family's lounge room.

The bevelled jade glass award for first place usually sat next to a framed photo of Cate, Christopher and Emma.

Cate picked up the photo and examined her younger, care-free features, those of her beaming daughter and the more studied smile from Chris.

Eight years. She shook her head at the familiar clutch of her heart. Was it really that long ago?

She kissed two fingers and pressed them lightly to the photo before placing the frame back in its space.

The gap next to it used to be filled by the perpetual trophy her mum and grandma brought home year after year for their winning family recipe. The same recipe Cate followed for this year's competition.

But she'd failed to win it back. For the first time.

Emma came up behind her and spoke in a reassuring tone —a reversal of roles, Cate thought.

"We can put my banana-loaf trophy up here. And next year you'll get the sponge trophy back and I'll win again so the two trophies can sit side by side."

"Em, don't worry about me. I've got to let go of the dream. Grandma and your great grandmother are sending out good vibes from the other side. 'It's just a cake,' I can hear them saying."

Emma gave her mother a peck on the cheek.

"Sooo." Emma clasped her hands together. "What did you think of the new boy in town?"

"Gus Fiorelli? I haven't given him a second thought," Cate said rather too quickly.

Emma's brown eyes sparkled. "You must have some sort of

opinion. He's hot."

Cate gave an unseemly chortle. "Really? Nah. Didn't notice."

"Come on, Mum, don't tell me you didn't drown a little in those deep blue eyes. For someone that old, he's hot as. I checked him out on the Internet—he's single."

Cate turned her back on the family photo—turned away from Chris, with his boyish good looks, straw-coloured hair and eyes almost the same as Emma's.

For the first time since Chris's death, she'd experienced a pleasant heady sensation when she'd thought about another man. Guilt prodded her with a big sharp stick.

"How do you know he's single? And before you start match-making, you should know I'm not interested."

Emma harrumphed. "It's been eight years, Mum. We've been a tight unit and we've battled through the hard times together. I don't think Dad would mind if you started seeing someone else. Give yourself permission to move on."

"Whoa, don't get ahead of yourself."

"Listen to me. Gus owns a couple of cafés in Melbourne. They're really cool—you should go online and take a look. I found an article in the Sunday paper. He's moved here for a new challenge. His wife died five years ago from cancer." Her voice softened. "Like Dad."

A stone thunked into a pond in Cate's stomach and sank rapidly to the bottom. She squeezed her eyes tight to stop the sting of fresh tears.

"We're both tired." Her words were heavy with exhaustion. "Let's talk about this tomorrow after the awards dinner."

As she dragged herself towards the bedroom, Cate wished tomorrow had come and gone, and that Gus Fiorelli would look less attractive in the light of a new day.

❧

THE AWARDS DINNER was the biggest event on the Webelong Valley CWA's annual calendar. Everybody who was anybody in the small country town, plus the surrounding dairy farms and outlying hamlets, scrabbled for tickets that were snapped up quicker than bluefin tuna at a Japanese fish market.

Cate had been to so many dinners with her mother and grandmother that she'd begun to feel jaded.

But tonight a kaleidoscope of butterflies busied themselves in her tummy. The late afternoon light seemed brighter and her senses sharper.

She even found herself humming a silly love song while she put on her makeup with more care than usual.

"Not bad, not bad at all," she told her reflection as she applied mascara to her long eyelashes. Her mother always told her to make the most of her best asset: "Green eyes go with green aquatic colours, Cate."

Tonight she wore a sleeveless, deep green A-line dress and replaced the Blundstones she wore to work at the family's tractor showroom with a pair of red patent-leather slingbacks. Emma looked gorgeous in a little black frock that enhanced her silken skin.

Arriving at the hall unfashionably early, they found their place cards on a table in the back corner. Cate didn't mind. She'd had her chance to shine and she'd blown it.

She wondered where Gus Fiorelli would be seated. If Charlotte had anything to do with it, he'd be on her lap stage side.

She checked the names on the place cards around her—all second- and third-place getters, except for Emma.

Gus arrived 15 minutes later. Right on time. Not that she'd noticed. Much.

"Charlotte's cut him off at the pass," Emma murmured despondently as she sucked on the lemon in her gin and tonic. "We'll never get to talk to him."

Cate didn't know what she wanted. She'd spent a restless

night worrying herself stupid about letting another man into the life she'd built with Emma.

They were a team, and Emma had only recently come through a bout of heavy-duty anxiety, which held her back from pursuing a baker's apprenticeship.

What if Gus wasn't interested in getting to know her? Or maybe Emma had got her research wrong and he was in a relationship?

Emma jiggled in her chair and kicked Cate under the table.

"He's coming over. I knew it. I knew he would."

"How's it going?" Gus sat in the empty seat beside Cate and picked up the place card. "Do you think Miss Ruby Walquist would be happy to swap places?"

Cate couldn't help the smile that spread from ear to ear. "She'd pay good money for the front row."

Emma bounced out of her seat faster than a sprinter out of the starting blocks. "Ruby just got here. I'll let her know."

She bounded across the room before Cate could stop her.

"She's a lovely young woman, you should feel very proud," Gus said, his smile softening.

Cate melted under the warmth of his gaze. At such close proximity she didn't need her glasses to confirm the colour of his eyes.

Definitely blue.

Before she totally lost her train of thought, Cate launched into a speech she'd practised in her head all day.

"I want to apologise for my behaviour yesterday," she said. "I'm not proud of the way I reacted to your cake winning first prize."

Gus raised a conciliatory hand. "I'm the one who should apologise. I entered at the last minute and didn't read the instructions. I probably wouldn't have followed them anyway. But that's not the point."

He wriggled his chair closer to Cate's, so that his mouth was enticingly close to her ear, and lowered his voice. "I laced the strawberries and cream with a truckload of Grand Marnier so the judges were probably tipsy when they cast the final vote. I didn't follow the rules and for that I must pay the price."

While Cate tried to absorb this information, Charlotte van der Kamp tapped at the mic and boomed, "Let's start the proceedings with the winners of the Queen Victoria sponge 'jam and cream filled' class."

Polite applause followed as Ruby Walquist claimed her third-place ribbon and medallion.

Charlotte cast her gaze to the back of the room and Cate breathed in deeply and braced herself for second place as all eyes focused upon her.

Sorry Mum. Please forgive me, Grandma.

"Second place goes to ... " Charlotte allowed a moment before Cate's fate was sealed.

"Gus Fiorelli.

"See you up there." Gus jogged to the stage amidst wild applause.

The commotion had barely subsided when Cate's name was called.

After handshakes and hugs from well-wishers she stumbled onto the stage in a daze, where a broadly grinning Charlotte handed her the soft-green tinted trophy that bore the names of her mother and grandmother. And now hers.

With shaking hands, Cate held the jade glass aloft by its deeper green base as Emma whooped and whistled from the audience.

Turning to Gus, she smiled into those seriously deep blue eyes.

"This really belongs to you."

Leaning towards her, his lips brushed her cheek. "There's always next year."

8

A NAME TO LIVE UP TO

SARA HARTLAND

J aded. The word seemed to fit the attractive brunette, who wasn't meeting anyone's gaze while she waited for her coffee.

Ben remembered that feeling. It used to dog his days as a corporate lawyer, but not anymore. These days he took his chances, embraced his opportunities and danced with life's ups and downs. Last week the woman had slipped out before he could act. He'd seen her in the park too, but at a distance. Today he was feeling lucky. His chief barista, Cassie, noticed him lurking, wiping down a bench that clearly didn't need cleaning. She finished making the woman's coffee and shot him an enquiring look.

He grabbed a lid and she passed him the cup, smiling. He turned it to see the name scrawled on the side.

"Wish me luck," he whispered.

Cassie grunted. "You don't need it."

Bravado pushed him around the counter.

"Beverley? Half-strength long black with a dash of cold water?"

The woman turned to him with a look of surprise. She

reached for the coffee and he went to pass it to her, fumbling a little. She grabbed for it and their fingers tangled. His shiver of reaction surprised him. She must have felt it too, pulling her hand back, now clasping the coffee.

Way to go, Romeo. Very smooth.

"I've double cupped it so it's not too hot. Is that all right?"

She glanced at him briefly and just smiled. *Damn, she wasn't going to answer.* He realised he desperately wanted to hear her voice.

"Beverley is an unusual name these days. Mine's Ben. Not unusual at all." He grinned but she missed it, shrugging the strap from her heavy shoulder bag back in place. Then she looked at him directly, her head tilted. *Those eyes!* He felt his world tip on its axis, then realised she was speaking.

"It's just my coffee name. Thanks." Her voice was low and musical but its effect hit him in the chest like a kick-arse espresso. She turned to go and he had to restrain himself from reaching out a hand to her arm to stop her.

"You mean it's not your real name? Aha, now I'm really curious."

She hesitated in the doorway. This time her smile was tinged with sadness. "Life's better with a few mysteries, don't you think, Ben?" She gazed at him and a smile ghosted her face before she dropped her eyes. "Thanks for the coffee."

He watched her walking down the street. The breeze caught the hem of her red and white polka dot skirt and it fluttered around shapely, pale legs as she disappeared into Joe's delicatessen. Maybe Joe knew her? He'd drop by with his nephews after school and quiz him. The boys were always ravenous then. He could feed them milkshakes and muffins before they hit the soccer field and team practice. He flicked his long fringe out of his eyes as a plan slowly formed.

~

LAURA WISHED she hadn't been so vague talking to that guy in the coffee shop. What was his name? She was flustered when he came out to give her the coffee. He was cute, with his too-long hair and his lean and lanky physique. She didn't sleep well these days and needed caffeine in her system before she could hold up her end of a conversation. And she was plain out of practice. Too many hours running her mother to hospital and medical appointments, and too many days alone since her mother had died.

Cancer was a bitch, but Laura thought hope was the worst. Every time her mum was in remission, Laura hoped it was gone. Then, when the spots on her lungs came back, the fall to despair felt like it came from higher and higher cliffs, not the bumps in the road Beverley called them. Laura stayed brave, stuffed down her anxiety and worked hard to be positive and upbeat. And in the end it didn't matter what either of them hoped. Her mum was gone.

And Laura was numb.

Getting through her days now required caffeine and low expectations. It saved disappointment. People died, boyfriends left, dream jobs ended, friends fell away. That was just life. Maybe tomorrow she'd manage a proper conversation. Baby steps.

As the coffee kicked in back at the house, Laura pushed aside her morose thoughts, dragged the wheelie bin to the back door and began filling it with the garage bags she'd neatly stacked. She avoided looking at the overgrown garden beyond the back patio. It could wait.

The charity shop people were due in an hour to assess the furniture. Before they came Laura had one job to do she'd been avoiding: cleaning out Beverley's bedside table. She was fine until she found the jade pendant, then the tears started again. Most of her mother's jewellery featured gemstones, but she hadn't worn the jade pendant since Laura was eight. Her geologist father, John, had given it to her mum shortly before he died in a coalmine collapse. Beverley never wore it because she believed jade opened the heart chakra and she didn't want to let go of her love for Laura's dad.

Laura lifted the pendant out of its velvet-lined box and tears dripped off her chin and were swallowed by the plush navy fabric. The jade's simple drop shape was sleek in her hand, and on impulse she slipped the chain around her neck and fastened it, tucking it beneath her T-shirt. The gem rested above her heart and felt warm against the skin, like it was meant to be there. Maybe it would help her heal? The thought and the weight of the pendant were soothing.

Two hours later the charity shop guy had arranged to come back with his truck another time and Laura had stripped the first of the garden beds of weeds. Feeling her skin tighten from too much sun, Laura retreated into the cool inside the old Queenslander cottage. She ate the spicy chickpea salad she'd bought at the delicatessen, surprised to find it tasty. She hadn't enjoyed food for a long time; Beverley could only tolerate bland dishes. Maybe the burst of outdoor activity had done her good.

Later, Laura taped closed another box of books for donation and decided she needed to get out of the house. The ticking clock was getting to her. Grabbing a novel from a series she used to enjoy, she tossed it into her bag and resolved to walk to the park, find a shady spot and read for half an hour. Some days it felt like she was in a bubble, moving through the world but not part of it. She'd just have to keep going through the motions until life started to feel real again. It was a shaky plan, but it was a plan.

Settling under a tree in the park, she inspected the book cover. Perhaps the racy novel might kick up her pulse. The hero was long and lanky and reminded her of someone. Laura read the back page description and memory clicked. The barista.

What was his name again? Ben? His smile was pretty cute and he'd tried hard. Noticing a cute male was a healthy sign, wasn't it?

Her reverie was shattered by a missile knocking the book flying. She was so startled she yelped. A small boy stopped running toward her, eyes huge. A soccer ball rolled to a stop in bushes nearby.

"I'm sorry. I didn't mean to." He looked scared and stopped a little bit away from her.

"Hey, don't worry about it. You just startled me." The child's face relaxed and he turned to yell behind him. "It's all right. I can get it."

Laura scrambled to her feet, picking up her book and the ball. She looked beyond the boy and recognised a familiar face.

Barista Ben jogged over and ruffled the hair of the boy, who looked about five. Another slightly older boy raced up to his side. Ben was wearing baggy sports shorts and a T-shirt that showed off a nicely defined chest. He had his cap on backwards and he looked relaxed and happy as he smiled at her.

"Beverley? Hi. Sorry about that. Andy and Travis get carried away. Did it hurt you?"

Laura shook her head. "No, just surprised me. And my name is actually ..."

Ben interrupted her by putting a hand up. "Nup, don't tell me. I've already got a name for you. It can be your park name, different to your coffee name. I'm calling you Jade, okay?"

"Why Jade?"

'Hmm. The colour of your eyes, the mystery, and you just seemed a bit ..." he hesitated and then shrugged. "To be honest, a bit jaded."

Laura flushed but laughed. He'd noticed her eyes. And her mood. A guy with emotional insight. *Why were all the good guys taken?* "Okay, fair enough. Are these your sons?" She was curious; he seemed too young for parenthood.

"Nah, these guys are my nephews. The one with the lethal kick is Andy, and the big fella is Travis." He slung an arm around each of their shoulders. "Say hi, guys." The boys mumbled greetings and both offered their hands to shake, which Laura did while hiding a smile. They were adorable.

"The boys and I just like to hang out in the park in the afternoons after school. Do you play soccer at all? You're welcome to have a kick with us if you'd like. We could use a fourth person."

Laura went to refuse but something about the challenging look on Ben's face made her turn to the boys. She tilted her chin.

"I don't know, you guys look like you know what you're doing. Would it be okay? I haven't kicked a soccer ball in a long time. But you'd better call me Laura. That's my real name."

The kids agreed happily. Ben smiled and Laura suspected she'd passed some kind of test. "Laura. I like it even more than Jade. Pleased to meet you."

He held out his hand and she hesitated. Ben was danger-ously attractive. Her plan was to sell the cottage and move back to Sydney. She didn't want dangerously attractive in her life right now. Or did she? When she reached out to take his hand, she had the strongest sensation of something shifting in the air, and the slide of his strong fingers curling around hers loosened a knot inside her chest. Ben's eyes darkened and a slow smile lifted his lips. Did he feel it, too?

The moment was broken when the smaller boy held out his hands for the ball and hopped from one foot to the other.

"It's pretty good fun, Laura. Do you want to see how far I can kick the ball?"

Ben laughed. "Andy, maybe you should let Laura have a go first."

Andy looked reluctant and Laura suppressed a grin. Ben whispered out of the side of his mouth, "He hogs the ball a bit, just sayin'." Andy overheard and looked cross until Laura dropped the ball on the ground and nudged it in his direction. Travis started running backwards to be in position to play.

The next hour rolled past with laughter and yells of encouragement. Ben tried to coach Laura in the finer arts of kicking the round ball and they ended up forming two teams and competing to be the first to score a goal.

Laura worked up a sweat and was beginning to tire when finally Travis put a ball into the net. Andy looked crestfallen but accepted a pat on the back from his uncle and a promise to return to the park later in the week.

"But we need Laura so we can play a game again. We can't do it with three people. Laura, will you come, too? Please, please, please?" He looked up at her with earnest big brown eyes. Ben stood behind him and mimicked Andy's desperate expression. "Yeah Laura, please?"

Laura laughed. "I suppose that could work out. Ben will have to text to let me know when." Andy and Travis gave each other a high five and Ben's slow smile rewarded her. *God, his smile was something.* Maybe it was the endorphins from the exercise, maybe it was the joyful company of little children, or maybe it was just Ben drawing her out, but this was the best day she could remember since she'd come back to care for her mother. The thought had her drawing in a sharp breath.

Ben noticed. "You okay?"

She nodded. "It's been fun. Thanks. I think I needed this."

He didn't say anything, just nodded and bent to gather up his backpack. It gave her a moment to brush the tears that threatened to spill from her eyes. She blew out a slow controlled breath. The sadness eased and lightness replaced it. She was reluctant to let it go so Laura turned to the boys. "Do you guys like ice-cream? I was thinking of getting some on my way home."

They turned to their uncle for his response.

"Sorry, I should have asked you first. Can I buy you ice-cream, too?"

Ben just laughed. "Thanks. I'd like that and so would the boys."

The boys knew the way to the shop and rushed ahead along the path, heeding Ben's call to wait for them at the corner to cross the road.

"Ben, thanks for including me in your afternoon. The boys are great. You have a lovely relationship with them."

"I'm glad you've enjoyed it as much as me." His voice lowered. "I was going to ask you out the next time you came in for a coffee, but running into you at the park gave me a chance to ruthlessly exploit their cuteness and energy for my evil purposes."

Laura laughed. "Evil, huh? That sounds interesting." *And thrilling*. Her pulse quickened. Ben stopped walking as the boys detoured to jump on playground equipment.

"Fair warning. In fact, I saw you here last week, so I was prepared to drag the kids here every afternoon until we ran into you. Was that wrong of me?"

'Seriously?' Her heart did a little flip.

"Yeah, well, to be honest, something about you said you might not go for the direct approach if I just asked you in the shop."

"You're probably right. I've been a bit of a recluse, looking after my mum. She passed away recently. Cancer. Beverley was her name." She'd not been able to speak about her loss yet to anyone new. It was a relief to tell someone and not fall apart. Ben was easy to talk to, fun and kind to children; pretty much the opposite of her ex who'd resented her attention to her mum and 'refused to put his life on hold' while Laura cared for her.

Beverley would have liked Ben, Laura realised, and unconsciously rubbed the jade pendant beneath her T-shirt. Was it wrong to feel attraction when she was so overwhelmed by grief she could barely get out of bed some mornings? Ben had been giving out signals, but would he still be interested now he knew she might be an emotional trainwreck?

"Ah, your mysterious coffee name. It's perfect. You get to say her name and hear other people speak it and she stays still part of your life even though she's gone. I'm so sorry about your mum. Cancer is a nightmare." He nodded towards the boys. "They lost their dad last year. Brain tumour. Dave was thirty-five. My sister, Evie, and I were already close, but I wanted to be a real uncle to the boys, not just some guy they see at Christmastime. I quit the Sydney rat race and opened the coffee shop. No regrets."

"Seriously?" Laura's heart immediately ached for the little boys and their mum, but she admitted to herself she was a little jealous they had Ben.

"Hey, I'm not a saint. I hated being a lawyer, but honestly, it is the best thing I've ever done. I can't take away their pain, but I can be here. I love my family and I love my life."

Wow, she thought. *Just wow.* Emotionally intelligent and self-aware? How was she supposed to resist that?

He bumped his shoulder against hers. "How are you doing? Do you have siblings?"

Laura swallowed the lump in her throat. "No siblings. It was just me and Beverley since my dad died when I was eight. I'm doing okay, just faking it until I make it. Some days good, some bad. Today was definitely a good day." She looked at him and smiled. "The best."

Ben took her hand in his and it felt so good that Laura felt different kinds of tears threaten: happy ones.

He smiled at her. "I'm so glad. Hey, I have a new park name suggestion for you. Jade isn't right for you, despite your lovely eyes. Want to hear it?"

She nodded.

"How about Joy?"

Laura tossed the idea around. It wasn't crazy. "That's quite a name to live up to. Are you offering to help me find mine?"

He raised her hand to his lips and pressed a quick kiss to her knuckles and she had to stifle a little sigh. She'd answer to any name if he did that to her lips.

"I'd like that."

She stopped walking and so did Ben. They turned to each other. His face was serious and slightly nervous. On impulse she stepped closer and reached to brush her lips against his. As kisses went it was almost chaste, but it packed a punch. His lips were warm and smooth and definitely worth exploring when they didn't have an audience. The boys looked amazed and Ben's look of surprise morphed into delight.

Laura smiled. "Then call me Joy."

9

THE JADE PRINCE

DIANNE INGLIS

Mya opened the door and cautiously peered outside. It was dark bar the light of the moon, the only sound the howling of a hyena far off in the distance. It was a huge risk, she knew, but she must see Sein before tomorrow. Tomorrow, when her fate was to be decided for her.

Pulling the door closed quietly behind her she crept along the path, bypassing the quarters where her potential suitors lay sleeping. Her maid, Htet, had delivered her message to Sein earlier that day. When she returned she assured Mya he would be waiting for her behind the large teak tree on the forest edge as the moon rose high in the sky.

It had rained in the afternoon, the usual torrential downpour for this time of the year. The sky was clear now though, thank goodness, the stars twinkling like diamonds and the moon bright enough to light her way.

Mya drew in a deep breath of the warm, humid air and stepped into the darkness of the forest, rounding the huge teak directly before her. *Please be here*, she silently prayed as her eyes adjusted to the dimness.

Sein was waiting. He opened his arms and she fell into them with a muffled sob. He held her close and gently caressed her hair. She could feel the pounding of his heart through his shirt and the quickness of his breath against her cheek. Their lips met in a kiss of fiery passion emanating from deep within. This was not simply lust. He was part of her core and had been since they had met six years ago, when he was a novice monk and she a student preparing for her role as future queen. Alone in the trusted environment of the monastery, no one had questioned the friendship between the shaved-headed youth and the young princess as they shared the lessons of Buddhism.

"We must run." She pulled back so she could look up at his face. "We must, Sein. We must run now so that we can be sure we will be together forever." She tugged his sleeve urgently.

Sein was shaking his head. He stroked her cheek and wiped the tears that remained.

"Mya, we run then we run forever. We can *never* stop running and your father would not rest until he found us and killed me for dishonouring both you and him. I *must* stay and fight for you."

"What good is *honour* if you are dead?" her voice caught on the words. "If we leave now we can be far away before the sun comes up and anyone realises we have gone. Sein, I *beg* you. Please do this for me. I *cannot* live without you. I would rather die. I saw them place the dagger with the hilt of jade in the ivory box today. The course is treacherous and the competition will be fierce!" She stepped toward the darkness of the forest and reached out her hand for him, willing him to follow. He stood fast.

"I *will* be the one to bring the jade dagger and lay it at your feet. I will be the one to claim you as my own and I will *do it with honour*." Sein spoke the last words through teeth clenched tightly. He took her outstretched hand and drew her to him, resting his chin atop her head, holding her close for a moment before propelling her gently away.

"Go home, my Mya. Rest, for tomorrow I will claim you as my bride." He reached into his pocket, drawing out a small hessian bag tied with string coiled about the top. "Promise me you will wear this. When I gaze up at you from the arena I want to see the glisten of the sun's reflection. It will give me luck, and you hope and faith that by day's end it will be me you are promised to forever." He turned her so that she faced the way she had come. "Now go."

Mya reached out to him but he stepped back just beyond her reach.

"I *will* be the victor." His voice was fierce. "There is *no* other option for me. I will make you proud to stand alongside me, knowing that I battled strongly for you." He stepped away and was quickly enveloped by the trees.

Mya crawled into bed and it was there, in the privacy of her room, that she unwound the twine holding the small bag closed. She withdrew a long pin, a cap covering the sharp point. On the other end was a stone of green embedded in a setting of the highest quality yellow gold. A jade. Mya knew the significance of this gift. The quest tomorrow was to be victorious in claiming the jade dagger and presenting it in exchange for her hand in marriage.

Mya sat poker still as her hair was pulled this way and that, Htet's hands twisting and twining as they pinned strands in a style becoming increasingly flamboyant with each pin inserted.

"This is an exciting day, my child." Mya raised her eyes to

meet her mother's, reflected in the mirror she sat before. She didn't feel excited. She felt sick and anxious. "You must put on a brave face and you must *look* the part of an excited bride waiting to meet her intended one. A man who will battle to prove his commitment and strength and passion for you."

"You mean a stranger who will win me as a prize, like a cow or a pig. Someone selected for me and not someone that I choose myself." Mya glared at her mother, shrugging away the hands entwining jewels and gold thread through her hair. "I won't do it. Mama, I *can't*. Please. Can you not talk to Papa, to the elders, and ask them—no, *tell* them—that I should be free to marry who I please?"

Soe was shaking her head. Her hand pressed down on Mya's shoulder, forcing her to remain in the chair. She beckoned with her head, and the hands creating the elaborate bouffant went back to work.

"It is the *way*, Mya. You know this is the way your husband is to be chosen. You think *you* know better? You think you are wiser in the way of marriage than are the elders, and we, your parents?" she shook Mya's shoulder, her frustration with her daughter clear on her face. "Ten fine men carefully selected. The strongest and bravest, who claims the sword with the jade hilt, *will* be the one for you."

Mya choked down a sob. The thought of living her life without Sein was impossible to comprehend.

"Your father will be along shortly to escort you to the arena. Enough of this. It is in the hands of the spirit gods now, and you *must* accept that it is so." Soe walked across the room, averting her eyes from her stricken daughter. The door clicked closed behind her.

Mya lifted her bowed head, her tear-filled eyes meeting Htet's own.

"Almost finished and then we get you dressed." Htet leaned forward. "It will be all right, I am sure. The spirits will favour you." Htet nodded assuredly, pulling the last strands of hair into place.

Mya reached into the pocket of her dress. Removing the hessian bag, she withdrew the jade pin and held it out to Htet.

"Please place this in the centre of my hair, Htet. High at the front for all to see that I embrace the jade that is to be my fortune."

Htet took the pin and stroked the green gem with her thumb. It would be a stunning finish to the elaborate hairstyle, and to the gown that lay across the bed ready for Mya to don. She nestled the pin into Mya's hair, the jade a stunning contrast to the black of her hair.

MYA COULD HEAR the roar of the crowd as she neared the arena. Htet straightened her gown before stepping back to allow Soe a final appraisal. Soe's eyes widened slightly as she spied the jade gem adorning her hair. She said nothing as Mya took hold of her father's elbow for the final walk to their seats at the ringside. There they would observe the battle of the suitors for her hand.

The noise subsided as they entered.

"His Royal Highness, King Shway, Queen Soe and the Princess Mya," a loud voice bellowed. The crowd cheered. This was an exciting day. The only child of the king and queen was due to marry. With no male heir, the tradition was for the strongest and bravest men in the country to prove their worthiness to marry the princess and produce an heir to succeed the throne on the king's death.

"Thank you," Mya murmured quietly as the courtier assisted her to her chair. Her mother sat to her left, her father to the right.

Drums rolled, gongs and cymbals clanged. An audible gasp

rippled throughout the stadium as the procession of suitors entered the arena. They were all strong with bare chests glistening from a mix of paint and oil applied by families proud that their sons were considered worthy of the princess.

One by one they approached the royal family and bowed deeply before moving toward the centre of the arena where the battle would play out.

Mya nobly nodded, forcing a smile as each approached, in the way that was expected. But she watched for just one man. As Sein drew closer her heart quickened. His name was spoken and then he stood before her. His chest was bare, as were the others. But this chest she knew more intimately, her fingers familiar with the firmness and each groove and ridge of muscle, her nose with his musky scent.

His expression was focused. Mya leaned slightly forward lowering her head in a regal bow. She raised her head meeting his eyes. Mya was sure he had spied the jade cushioned in her hair. Luck for him, faith for her.

THE SUITORS WAITED in the centre of the arena like nervous colts, moving from one foot to the other. The prize was worthy of the fight. Princess Mya was exquisite, with her long black hair that shone like silk, skin translucent in its beauty and mouth that bore full lips made for kissing. Only one man *knew* her, of her hopes and dreams, her fears and passions. Only one man had touched her physically and spiritually.

The crowd hushed as the large gong sounded loudly, heralding the start of the competition. Nine men stood, chests thrust forward, stances strong and powerful. For them winning was the accolade regardless of the prize.

Sein stood quietly. Mya could see his fists clenched by his sides and the determined concentration on his face. He did not partake in the jostling and bravado the other men displayed. He was focused on winning his princess.

The gong sounded once more. Any joviality faded quickly as one large boulder after another was moved from one pile to the next. The sun burned and sweat ran in rivulets down backs and chests. Muscles enlarged as blood coursed to nourish the straining limbs. Sein had trained hard, knowing his full strength would be tested. He was first to move his pile of rocks and Mya had to sit on her hands to stop from clapping with glee. It was early, yet with still more challenges to come the battle was just beginning.

Eight remained. Man faced man balanced on a narrow beam barely wide enough for one foot. Beneath them a writhing mass of hissing vipers offered only one fate to the loser. Legs braced and toes curled, gripping the timber. Each man was armed with a long bamboo pole.

Three loud gongs penetrated the air. A loud clash as bamboo struck bamboo. Muscles bunched as brute strength met brute strength. Pushing, jostling, trying to force the other off balance. The first one plunged. Mya strained to see who it was. She could not. The pit at the far end was too far away.

The second fell, his screams loud as the vipers struck. He was pulled from the pit and lay alongside while someone doused him with water. Was he alive? Mya could not tell. Nausea rose in her throat. Had this man died ... because of her?

Four fighters remained facing each other. Another two men resting, awaiting the next round. Where was Sein? From this distance, she couldn't be sure. *Please*, Mya silently prayed. He *must* be one to continue to the next round. A third man fell, then a fourth.

There he was. Mya sagged back into her chair, unaware she had perched on the edge and was straining forward searching for the familiar figure among the four remaining. As they approached the grandstand, Mya could see he was injured.

Blood oozed from a wound on his forehead. Impatiently he swiped it away, sending crimson droplets into the air. The blood mixed with the paint now smeared across his chest, still heaving from the exertion.

Their reprieve was short. Wild boars in cages were carried into the arena, long poles projecting from either end carried on the shoulders of four warriors. The squeals of outrage made Mya's blood run cold. Their horns battered at the bamboo constraining them.

Each remaining suitor was handed a short dagger and a club carved from wood. The dagger was plain with a handle of worn metal. The sharp edge caught the sun, a bright reflection glistening off the blade. It was similar in shape to the jade handled dagger, but the comparison stopped there. The jade dagger was an artful masterpiece. This dagger's purpose was pure function.

The warriors carrying the cages settled them to the ground with a grunt. With pointed sticks, they prodded the animals within, guaranteeing that angry beasts would be released. The men would fight not only for the princess, but for their very lives.

Sein stood with legs slightly apart, balanced on the balls of his feet, poised to react. He looked up at the grandstand. Mya's eyes were trained on him. She touched her fingers to her lips, reached up to caress the jade adornment, and then placed her open hand over her chest.

"I love you," she mouthed.

He turned back toward the cage. The warriors loosened the ties holding it closed. He breathed deeply. His hand opened and closed around the handle of the dagger, his eyes now firmly focused on the cage ahead.

The beast burst forth from its enclosure with a roar, head tossing this way then that. It's nostrils flared as it surveyed the scene. Sein was directly ahead. The boar pawed at the ground as it lowered his head. It charged.

Sein struck out with his club, knocking the boar to the side. He swung around quickly to once again face it full on. The boar was enraged now, saliva spraying from his mouth, a low, guttural sound coming from deep in his chest.

The club swung again. The beast stumbled. Its chest smacked Sein in the abdomen, knocking him to the ground. He rolled to the side, fumbling for his dagger, just out of reach in the red dust. As his hands curled around the handle he felt the earth shudder under the pounding feet. He rose to his knees, stared momentarily into wild red eyes and flaring nostrils before thrusting the blade upward into the boar's neck. The boar staggered then collapsed to its knees, blood spurting in a wide arc.

Mya rose to her feet along with the rest of the crowd. Her mother cautioned her with an arm on hers or she would have joined in the cheering.

The boar fell sideways to the ground, his leg jerked several times and then he was still. Sein sank back onto his haunches and wiped the blade of his dagger against the leg of his pants before letting it drop to the dirt.

He did not move.

Get up, Mya willed him, *get up*! He had to be the first to the ivory box on the pillar before her father.

The crowd roared again, drawing Mya's attention away from Sein. She looked up as the remaining suitor threw himself onto the back of the writhing mass circling him. He grasped the horns and jerked them backwards, exposing the pulsing veins in the sweaty neck. He plunged in the knife and moved it back and forth in a sawing action. The beast stumbled and fell, taking the suitor down with him.

Sein was on his feet but something was wrong. He staggered a few steps then fell to his knees once again. Mya took a step forward and felt the tug of her mother's hand on the back of her dress. She swiped it away. Fear clutched at her throat.

The second man was crawling away from his felled animal now, heading toward her.

Please Sein, please! Mya's hands were clasped in prayer as she propelled all her mental energy toward him. He rose to his feet again as the second competitor drew up alongside.

Mya could see Sein's determination as he moved forward to take the lead. His eyes fixed on hers. His competitor's hand grasped at his shoulder. Sein turned, pushing it away. His competitor fell to the ground.

King Shway stood as Sein neared. The king lifted the jade dagger from the ivory box and with both hands held it out. Kneeling, Sein carefully laid it at Mya's feet. She bent, picking it up, and gently touched it to his left shoulder, then his right, claiming him as her jade prince.

Sein stood, faltering, his body weakened. Mya's hand grasped his, steadying him. Together they raised the dagger as the crowd roared its approval.

10

THE BOY THIEF

JEFF KENNEALLY

Her eyes closed, Mariah sniffed again, long, savouring, wondering. The smell of cinnamon was clear, as was anise. Perhaps cardamom, too. A passerby jostled her. Just what she expected in the souk as the morning picked up its busiest trade. Even walking in a marketplace was exciting in this land. The spice-filled baskets before her, artistically beautiful in their reds, oranges and browns, a kaleidoscope of Arab exotica.

Not roughly, Mariah felt herself pushed to one side. A man, skin darkened from a life lived in harsh sun, stared at her almost challengingly. One yellowed tooth protruded from his lower gum, another from the gum above. He stood close, his breath sweeping away the pleasantness of the market in an instant. He was here to trade and she was not. She quickly moved on.

The docks at the street end were noticeably quieter. Most of the fishing fleet was out and would not return until long after Mariah was back in her hotel. A few dhows were fastened to ancient pillars, their angular lines curving into ornate beak heads, compelling her eyes to follow from one ship to the next.

They lapped gently as a few men roamed without urgency about the decks or along the wharf.

At the foot of the nearest ship, a young boy stood arguing with a very elegantly dressed man. He was no fisherman. The boy at once contradicted, partly deferring to the man yet somehow appearing defiant. He could not have been more than twelve years old, yet he spoke with a confidence and authority beyond his years. Mariah moved closer, trying to remain unnoticed, intrigued by the exchange. The words meant nothing to her, but it was clear the boy was up to the challenge.

The boy turned away, leaving behind a sweeping gesture of appeal. As he passed Mariah, his olive skin looked fair, pure in fact. His dress was not of some scrubby street urchin and she wondered who he was. He moved quickly into the souk and was gone. She turned back to the older man, also staring after the boy.

With him gone, the man sighed. There was a sadness about him. He looked up and their eyes met. His face was curious at her interest in him. She took in his thin beard, the tiny triangle of hair beneath his lip. He spoke to her in Arabic. She couldn't reply, offering only a gesture of incomprehension.

"The boy, he is wrong but he is right," he said in perfect English.

His words puzzled her. She had little chance to ponder, transfixed by his alluring gaze. He gave her the slightest bow of his head before turning away.

She watched him go, still unable to speak. *Well done girl, paralysed by a look.*

Not just paralysed, melted.

She returned to the souk, making her way along the next laneway. This was entirely different, with elegant fabric rolls spilling from the stalls, their softness surpassed only by the ornate colours and patterns. A few shopkeepers made gestures inviting her to trade but she gently shook her head. Nobody pushed the point; she was a tourist, not a buyer.

She thought again of the elegantly dressed man, his penetrating brown eyes drawing her into some long funnel she had felt herself willingly pouring into. Loneliness had become her accepted life. Not for a long time had feelings for a man stirred within her. Yet this stranger in this faraway land was doing just that. She wished he had not turned away and imagined him crossing to her, holding her.

She found herself outside a small jewellery stall and was spellbound by the ornate golden pieces inside the window. Many had glorious stones, most of which she could not recognise but yearned to own. Necklaces, some simple, some complex and intricate, as if intended only for royalty to wear. Not for her then. She smiled wryly.

The boy appeared at the doorway, his interest in something within apparent. This time he remonstrated with the storekeeper, insistent about something. His finger pointed repeatedly at the much taller Arab barring his entry into the store. The storekeeper gestured to the boy to leave, clearly denying something. The boy took a step back and glared. He wasn't scared at all. Instead his face was a mask of determination.

Satisfied the boy had been warned off, the storekeeper turned back into his store. Mariah thought the exchange was over and was considering following the boy when he darted forward into the shop. Seconds later a crashing sound emanated, followed almost instantly by a loud, enraged cry. The window, filled with jewellery pieces, allowed little view into the shop. The shopkeeper's form could be partly seen sprawled on the floor, a cabinet lying atop him. He thrust it aside as he fought to right himself from his prone position.

A movement caught her eye as the boy appeared in the doorway. His expression was different, no longer simply defiant. His eyes wide, he scanned urgently left and right. For a fraction of a second he looked at Mariah before he set off. She watched him for a few steps.

A cry from behind made her start and she turned to see another Arab bearing down on the scene. Taller than the shop-keeper, a jagged scar on his cheek marked him, his appearance menacing, threatening. His long white thobe and red and white ghutra were unsuited to running but his scowling face said he was going to try. He yelled after the boy. As he neared Mariah his hand disappeared into his robe only to return partly concealing a glistening silver object.

A knife.

Its blade curved toward the tip, sinister and with clear intention. In an instant Mariah's mind fought the realisation the boy must be a thief. That was why he had caused this trouble in the shop.

Yet he didn't seem like a thief.

She had only an instant before the man launched himself after the boy, still bellowing. A reflex action, one that surprised her as much as the giant Arab pursuer, brought her arm up against several large silk rolls leaning against the shop wall. Mariah pushed and they fell heavily, directly across the man's path. Intent on the boy ahead, he realised too late and stumbled on them. Unable to check his momentum, he fell, sprawled facedown in the jewellery shop doorway. At that moment the shopkeeper appeared, himself still enraged. He kicked at the giant blocking the doorway, gesturing for him to get up and continue the pursuit.

The boy was in serious trouble.

Trouble that worsened. He hadn't escaped passed more than a few shops in the crowded lane when, looking back over his shoulder, he collided directly with an old man. Despite his frailty, the man staggered but somehow managed to remain on his feet. The boy rebounded sideways and fell into a stack of baskets. He was on his feet almost in one movement but had lost his head start. Instead of immediately running he wasted precious seconds looking around the baskets, searching. But, he knew his time was up as the giant regained his feet across the laneway.

He ran again, disappearing into the crowd. His two pursuers remained visible longer as the crowd parted, not able to absorb them as easily as it did the boy.

Mariah's heart was racing. She exhaled slowly through pursed lips at the realisation she had, for no clear reason, put herself in harm's way. She felt something for this boy, she knew not what.

Fortune had perhaps favoured her, but she was not one to push her luck. It was time to leave this area.

She took only a few steps before stopping to look down at the scattered baskets. Something had held the boy's interest, even as he ran for his life. What could be that important? She knelt quickly, pretending to rub an injured ankle. Her eyes roamed the ground but saw only the dust of the laneway.

And a glint of gold.

Pushing a basket aside she found his reason. A gold chain with a fine oval pendant attached. It was not nearly as ornate and intricate as many were in the window across the street. This was far simpler, yet instinctively she knew more valuable. In the centre of the pendant rose a darker object. Her arm slid forward surreptitiously, and she clasped the pendant. Her hand closed around it just as the storekeeper appeared, standing over her. He spoke, angrily she thought, and waved around him. Fearing he was blaming her for the mess she stood up, nodding. She continued nodding as she backed away. His look scared her but, after taking only one further step after her, he stopped and irritably gestured for her to leave.

She did.

Mariah had only one thought now, to escape to the safety of her hotel room. Clutching the necklace, she walked quickly through the market laneway until once again she felt safely anonymous. At least, as anonymous as she could be in the middle of an Arab souk. Curiosity was overwhelming her, tinged by the nagging realisation she couldn't simply return to her hotel.

She turned into a smaller side laneway. There were few people, none of them interested in her. Holding her hand close she opened it slightly, enough to see the jewel. She almost gasped. The gold was ornate enough, the stone was beautiful. It was dark green and yet it wasn't. As she moved it, the shifting light made it appear lighter then darker, striped then almost solid. Jade, she thought, mostly since that was the only green stone that came to mind. This was clearly something special to the boy, more than just something to steal. Who was he? Could he really be nothing more than a thief?

Holding the jewel now made Mariah feel in more danger than during the market scuffle. Why on earth had she picked it up? *Maybe I should report it to the local authorities somehow?*

She breathed fast; excitement arose. *Perhaps I could return it to the Arab. He knew the boy!*

Her attention was drawn further along the lane, where it took a moment to recognise the black and yellow bisht the boy wore. He looked like he was waiting, but for what? *Or who?*

This boy was dressed too well for a thief, his manner too confident. Instinct drove her as she walked toward him. He looked up and down the lane expectantly but without fear. As she neared, he focussed on her, his eyes narrowing as if trying to recall her.

His expression became fearful. The boy straightened, his arm sliding inside his robe, immediately finding the tiny dagger hidden there.

Mariah froze as the knife appeared. Of course he would not see her as a friend. He was being chased, fighting for his very life. She stopped, suddenly realising her foolishness and danger again. His eyes were fixed on her, distrustful and wary. She had to remember he was a boy and she was worse than a stranger, she was a foreigner.

His eyes shifted from Mariah to behind her. Compelled, she followed their direction over her shoulder and gasped. The giant Arab and the storekeeper were in their lane approaching them. They walked slowly, grinning with the knowledge their prey was trapped. The lane must have no way out.

Maybe they wouldn't notice her again? That thought was discarded as soon as it was born. She stood out and it could be no coincidence, her being here again. She clutched the jewel tightly. That alone guaranteed her demise.

Unable to take her eyes from her hunters, she shuffled backward away from them. The boy must have sensed by now that she was the least of his problems. They stood beside each other, no escape for either. Mariah watched both men continue their slow approach. The storekeeper had lost none of his anger. The giant, on the other hand, was grinning. He was enjoying this. His arm hung by his side, the long dagger all too apparent.

Mariah glanced at the boy, wondering what he was thinking. He didn't look as if he had an escape plan. For a mere boy of maybe twelve, he was remarkably composed. Not panicking, he surely felt at least some fear. Perhaps hers was enough for them both.

The giant Arab made no secret of the long dagger he held. He showed it gleefully, sadistically, to the two before him, savouring the joy of certain imminent victory. Mariah's knees felt weak and she wondered if they would buckle before she was slain.

A voice called out behind the two men. They all looked, including the two Arabs closing in on them. Two more men had entered the lane. Outwardly they looked little different to the first two.

Their two hunters turned to face the newcomers. Four daggers now pointed at each other, the fight inevitable between them. The four faced each other, crouched as fighters, gently swaying lightly on their feet, poised to strike. The giant was no longer smiling, having found two worthy adversaries. They all moved cautiously, warily, each seeking the right moment to strike at an opponent.

Yet two more men entered the laneway, then a third. Mariah suddenly felt despondent. Her pursuers had reinforcements just in time and the balance of power shifted again. Her demise had re-emerged from false hope.

Instead, though, their two pursuers stood straighter, their arms held out as if they sought to avoid the fight. The newcomers, still poised to fight, moved to one side as the last man to enter the lane came forward. He spoke but Mariah could not hear his voice. He pointed at the two men then gestured towards what Mariah assumed were his own men.

Both pursuers bowed their heads slightly and nodded. Even the giant man seemed suddenly cowed. Both backed against one side of the laneway then slowly moved sideways past the others. By the time they reached the end of the lane they had turned and moved quickly away.

Perplexed, her surging adrenaline beginning to fade, Mariah suspected her knees would suffer a similar fate. The thumping in her chest continued as she willed her breathing to slow again.

With the pursuers gone, the other three approached them. For an instant, it occurred to her they may have just changed one set of hunters for another. The boy took a step forward. The man in front, the leader, walked toward him. As he drew closer the boy launched himself into his outstretched his arms.

Suddenly awareness struck. She knew this man. It was her handsome man from the docks. His dress wasn't distinctive beyond being of great quality but his striking face certainly was, her memory of it vivid.

He pushed the boy back and held him out before him. They spoke. Rather he spoke and this time the boy seemed far more willing to listen, simply nodding at points. Gently he pushed the boy to one side and approached Mariah.

"Greetings again. I am," he hesitated for a moment, "Rasheed." He turned slightly and gestured. "Let me introduce my son, Hakeem."

Clearly the man was no threat to her and Mariah wondered what he would want from her.

As if reading her thoughts, Rasheed continued.

"My son tells me you helped him in the marketplace when he was being chased. I saw for myself you standing by him facing danger together. I am eternally grateful for this. Why would you do these things for a stranger, a mere boy?"

Mariah tried to speak but had to swallow twice to moisten her throat.

"My name is Mariah. I'm just a tourist. My husband," she sniffed, suddenly sad, "he died and I'm trying to fulfil his wish to live my life again." This man was disconcerting. His handsomeness this close was consuming her, the presence he exuded stirring feelings she had long thought gone from her life. She glanced at the boy and remembered the question she had been asked.

"I was certain your boy was no thief and was in great danger. It just felt right helping him."

Suddenly she recalled the necklace and held it out, hand open. Both boy and father stood agape, staring at it. Rasheed reached out and took it. The light moved through the gem as he held it up.

"This belonged to the boy's mother and her mother before. It was stolen from us and Hakeem has spent much time finding it." He looked upward for a moment and sniffed before continuing.

"I too lost my love. This stone is what we have left of her." Rasheed looked at the woman before him. The whiteness of her skin, eyes that themselves could be carved from jade. Proud, intelligent. She was beautiful, he suddenly realised. His saddened heart too, stirring in a way long forgotten.

"Perhaps Amina has spoken to me one last time through this stone." *Perhaps I should find out,* he told himself. "Will you join me in my home to celebrate its return and my son's life?"

"I would very much like that."

11

THE JADED RAKE

FIONA MARSDEN

J ulian Thorne was angry.

He was smiling, but Lissy had known him all her life and she recognised the signs: the way the corners of his mouth tucked in; the stormy glint in his heavy-lidded eyes; and the almost indolent way he sat on the low armchair, long muscular legs stretched across the luxurious carpet of his library. Julian never slouched. That seeming relaxed pose masked a tension that could snap at any moment. Heaven help the one engulfed in the maelstrom that would follow.

Lissy stiffened her back, clutching her beaded reticule with shaking fingers, for she was the one in the storm's path this day.

"Why are you here, Felicity? You are supposed to be residing at Thornedale Hall."

"Surely my place is at your side, husband."

If anything the tension rose, yet he barely moved. Only a slight twitch of one pale, elegant hand on his thigh, the faint lift of a well-defined black brow, showed his disturbance.

"You were sent to Thornedale in disgrace. There you were to wait until such time as I deemed it convenient to join you."

"And when would that be? I have been immured in your home for well-nigh three months."

"Bored, Felicity? I would think you needed the rest after your constant racketing around London during the season." His gaze dropped to her waist. "Are there no consequences to show for your misbehaviour?"

Her grip tightened, the beads cutting into her flesh. "If you wish to know if I'm increasing, the answer is no."

"Something to be grateful for. Your mama should have taught you the importance of ensuring your lord's progeny be provided before you introduce a bastard into his household."

"I'm aware that your only purpose in wedding me was to secure an heir."

"Something you have failed to do in the twelvemonth since we married."

"If you spent more time in your marital bed and less in that of your mistress, perhaps it might have some possible chance of happening."

"My mistress?" His brows rose in unison over eyes that had lost their indolence.

"Lady Orford. Everyone knows you spend your time with her to the neglect of your wife."

"Were you feeling neglected, Lissy? Is that why you played your dangerous games with young Belmain?"

His use of her nickname almost disarmed her. She stiffened her spine. There was no reason to believe he meant to be kind, any more than he'd really fallen in love with her that late summer's day twelve months ago.

"I was humiliated. Dismissed as unimportant and unworthy of notice."

"As my wife, as the Countess of Lydgate, you have a place in society unequalled."

"Perhaps if I had the support of my husband, instead of his obvious indifference, society would treat me with respect. If my husband has no thought of my dignity, it is hardly to be expected that others might see me with different eyes."

"You should have thought of that before dallying with young Belmain."

"I let him kiss me. Once. It was wet and slobbery and unpleasant. At least it gained me a few minutes of your attention."

Julian was silent, his eyes steady on hers. Lissy shifted uneasily.

When she'd been a child, Julian, orphaned in his teens and with a younger sister, had been the godlike neighbour who petted her and gave her sweets. On many occasions when he resided at Thornedale Hall he had taken her up in front of him on his large black stallion and galloped across the fields until she was breathless with exhilaration.

The years since had changed him into a world-weary rake, who found little joy in anything beyond his appreciation of a fine horse or a fine wine. Or perhaps a beautiful woman. Something Lissy was not. She could not help the sigh that escaped.

He seemed to relax, his hand brushing a long black lock back from his wide brow. "I regret your dalliance was such an unpleasant experience. I had not realised you were so desperate for attention."

"Surely not surprising, my lord. We were never in company. With each other."

"You expected me to dance attendance on you day and night?"

"With your other commitments I would be foolish to expect you to attend my bed. It would have been pleasant to have your company at occasional balls and routs and for my debut at Almack's after our wedding."

"You never seemed to miss me."

"You hardly encouraged me to hang on your sleeve."

"No. I suppose I didn't. I wasn't used to it. Lucretia never desired my company for such events."

Lissy's heart pinched at the mention of his first wife. Lucretia Thorne had been astonishingly beautiful. Her dark hair curled riotously around a haughty face with brown eyes that sparked with defiance at any attempt to control her wild behaviour. She could have married a duke, but she chose Julian Thorne.

That had been seven years ago, when Lissy had been but a child. She had begged her nurse to put her light brown hair into curl papers, but the fine sun-bleached strands never held, and there was little she could do about her snub nose with its sprinkle of freckles, and pale, indeterminate green eyes. The freckles at least had faded, but her small straight nose had developed none of the character indicative of a proud beauty.

After his marriage, Julian only intermittently visited his home until Lucretia's death, riding her husband's stallion for a dare and breaking her neck. He came more often then, throwing wild parties, but the neighbourhood saw little of him.

Her mama had warned her not to trespass in the wood that crossed the boundary of the two properties for fear of encountering one of the wild young men. Instead, she had encountered the Earl himself.

Lissy bestirred herself from her memories. "What is your decision, my lord?"

"Decision?" He drew his legs closer, sitting upright in the chair.

"Do I stay or do I go?"

He waved a hand, the greenstone ring catching the light. "Stay. For the moment. I will be attending a rout at Lord Orford's residence tonight. You may accompany me, or not, as you please."

This was laying down a challenge with a vengeance. If she stayed at home she was acknowledging her defeat. If she went she would see her husband flirting with his mistress. "If you have no objection, I would wish to attend."

His brows rose but he didn't speak.

She essayed a nonchalant tone. "I have been many months out of society. It would be foolish to miss such an opportunity."

"You should rest this afternoon. You look hagged to death." He stood, moving close so his presence loomed. "Missing me?"

She tilted her chin to meet his gaze without flinching. "Unlikely, my lord. I hardly saw you when I resided in London, so it made little difference being absent from your company. The journey fatigued me. The roads were rough and the post house noisy."

"A rest will do you good. I will send to the chef for a light meal to be sent up."

"Such consideration."

His mouth curled with genuine humour. "It would be a poor beginning to have you faint at your first outing in several months. The gossips would have a field day."

Lissy clamped her lips together, determined not to demean herself with a slanging match. Much he cared for gossip. She swept from the room, aware of the low rumble of laughter from her husband.

HANDING his young wife into the coach that evening, Julian took note of her appearance. The jade silk suited her colouring and deepened the unusual colour of her eyes. He had never thought of Lissy as a beauty though she pleased his eye. It had been other qualities that drew him to her that warm summer day a little more than a twelvemonth ago.

He had been bored beyond discretion with his guests and had only wanted to escape. His visitors had made themselves at home with his food and liquor and the fancy pieces they'd procured for their entertainment. Julian let them play. He had little desire for anything but finding the bottom of his glass. Women had long since ceased to interest him. Until Lissy appeared in his woods, hot and dishevelled and holding a grey-muzzled spaniel with a determined grip.

He'd dabbled in women a little after his first wife's death, if only to remind himself that he was a man, not a cuckold without the means to pleasure a woman, but it had soon palled. He was as jaded as Lissy had declared in their final argument before her banishment. No trust. No love to give. She had seen right through his pose of indifference to the truth.

He'd lost more than his youthful idealism at the hands of a wanton shrew of a wife. It had been a quick disillusionment thrust on him in a very public manner. He'd learned to protect himself, but at what cost?

The coach halted outside Lord Orford's townhouse. Lissy had more courage than he expected, for he had thought she would refuse to attend. He'd made too many mistakes in his handling of his bride.

"Come, Lissy." He helped her down from the coach, ensuring she didn't step in the muck. She hesitated to take his hand, perhaps afraid of the warmth that seeped through the gloves. It had startled him that first time in the woods. He'd really looked at her then, seeing not the child he'd been fond of, but the young woman who'd looked at him with worshipful eyes. It had struck him to the heart.

She no longer looked at him with that innocent adoration, when she looked at him at all. He could not blame anyone but himself. He'd driven her away with his determined indifference. He'd reacted to the scandal with all the disdain and contempt learned from his dealings with Lucretia. He should have listened to her three months ago. Nay, twelve months ago, when Lissy declared her love and he'd responded by distancing himself. Had he been afraid of a girl of seventeen?

LISSY CLUNG to Julian's hand, grateful for the heat that crept along her veins and warmed the chill in her aching heart. They had arrived late to the party, so would not have to meet their hosts in the receiving line at the top of the stairs. The servant announced them and the buzz of conversation halted for a brief moment before breaking out anew.

"It is not so bad, surely."

He was looking at their hands, at where her fingers were digging into his wrist. She released him immediately, feeling heat flood her cheeks. People were staring. She forced a smile and nodded at some acquaintances. They nodded back with polite smiles and she thought perhaps it would not be so bad. So long as Julian remained at her side.

She had been chatting with a group of young matrons like herself when she realised that Julian had moved away and was nowhere to be seen. Their hostess had remained out of sight, though Lord Orford stood talking amiably with a group of men.

Excusing herself, she made her way from room to room, seeking Julian's tall figure. Obeying some instinct, she looked up the stairs to the private part of the house. Voices grew distinct as she approached the top of the stairs, and they were there, only a few steps along the hallway, out of sight of those below.

Lady Orford smiled up at Julian, her hand resting protectively on her stomach, murmuring something in a low voice. Even with the disguising petticoats, Lissy could see the woman was with child.

She stepped back but it was too late. The woman had seen her, her eyes widening and alerting Julian to another presence.

"Lissy? Are you spying on me?"

"I couldn't find you." She tilted her chin. "I see you take

your own advice to heart. Lady Orford already has the two required heirs, so surely Lord Orford will forgive the introduction of your bastard into his household."

Julian's brows lowered and Lissy froze with fear at the icy look in his eyes. She stepped back and back again, into thin air.

Her name appeared wrenched from Julian's mouth and then she was falling, tumbling down the carpeted stairs. She could hear screams, but her own voice was mute, the taste of blood in her mouth and pain striking at her from all directions.

Something exploded in her head and darkness engulfed her, blurring the agony. She sank into it gratefully.

"LISSY. LISSY, PLEASE."

Julian's voice. He sounded desperate when she expected him to be angry. Angry at her words. Angry at creating a scandal in front of half the ton.

She forced her eyes open and winced at the light. There was a blur of movement and the candle shifted to one side.

"Are you in pain? Where does it hurt?"

She smiled at the foolishness of the question. "Everywhere."

"The doctor cannot find anything broken."

"I daresay I am merely bruised and a little battered. My head hurts."

"You hit it on the statue at the base of the steps." Gentle fingers brushed above her ear. "There is a lump."

"I always did fall easy."

Her eyes finally focused on Julian's face. His lips curved up and his eyes softened. "Like a floppy doll. I remember. I suppose that saved you from worse damage."

She didn't recognise the room. "Where are we?"

"In Lady Orford's private sitting room."

Lissy pushed herself up. "I can't stay." Pain shot like lightning behind her eyes and she collapsed.

A woman's voice spoke. "Would you like me to leave, Julian?"

"Not yet."

Tears pricked Lissy's eyes and tracked down her cheeks. "How could you?"

Julian wiped the moisture with his fingertips. "It's time to explain. I know you don't feel well, but it can't wait."

"Please don't send me away again."

"It will be all right, Lissy. You must listen. Gabby and I are only friends."

Lissy stared up at the two faces hovering in the light of the candle. "Only friends? But everyone ..."

"Everyone is wrong."

Lady Orford leaned forward, her face resolving into clarity. "It's true, child. My husband strayed and Julian comforted me. But that is all. This child is the proof that my marriage is recovering. It was news I wished to share with my friend."

Julian's hand gripped Lissy's and she turned to him. "Was it Lucretia?"

"How did you know?"

"I used to sneak into your woods to find Dobby and I saw her in the summerhouse sometimes. But never with you."

The woman faded into the distance. "I will leave you together. No one will disturb you."

Lissy lay in silence, staring at Julian. His eyes were the grey of a bleak winter's day, but she lacked to the courage to ask the question. Though she had little to lose. "Did you love her?"

"Lucretia?"

"Gabby."

"Gabby and I are good friends. We had to watch our partners flaunt their affair and so we understand each other. I have known Gabby since she was schooled with my sister in Bath.

She was heavy with her third child when the affair began. She lost the child, so to have another is a great joy."

"Lucretia was a fool."

His mouth twisted in a half smile. "You say that with great authority."

"She had you. Why should she seek love elsewhere?"

"Perhaps because she did not possess my heart. I was mad for her, true enough. She was beautiful and wild and every man wanted her. I had to possess her, to win out over all the other men. But when she strayed I found that it was mostly my pride that suffered. My heart recovered too quickly for it to have been truly engaged."

"How sad."

"I was young and stupid. Too young."

Her heart contracted, the pain far worse than that in her head. "I suppose I'm too young. And stupid."

"I think you were wiser than I was. You knew that it was love that mattered. You gifted it to me and I treated it with contempt."

His face tightened, and she yearned to comfort him. "I didn't understand. I thought at first you loved me too. Then everyone told me you only wished for an heir."

"You listen to everyone too much."

"Wasn't it true? You did not seem to have any affection for me beyond that of a foolish child you had known forever."

"That day in the woods you were like an angel come to save me from my despair. But I was afraid to give you power over me. It seems, when it comes to affairs of the heart, it is I who need teaching. I looked into those jade eyes and knew you were everything I ever wanted but didn't deserve. I expected it to be taken from me. So, I kept my distance."

His gaze captured hers and she saw all she could ask for in the depths of his stormy eyes. "You love me?"

"More than life. But I cannot hope for your love to have

survived after I treated it so brutally. When you fell tonight I knew I had almost lost the one thing that gave my life meaning."

She stroked his cheek. "How could I not love you? I've loved you all my life, even when you were a jaded rake seeking to ravish me in the woods."

"You responded so beautifully to my kiss. So innocent, yet with such passion."

She lowered her lashes, shy at the memory of her response. "Perhaps I loved you as a woman at that moment."

"My sweet wife." His mouth lowered to hers, brushing a kiss, so gentle, so full of tenderness, it filled her heart. "A jade-eyed girl for a jaded rake."

12

SILVER BULLET

HELENA MORRISON

Pushing up from his desk, Harry strode to the door and wrenched it open. "I repeat, Mr Jones, I am not taking your case. Now if you don't mind, I have work to do."

Jones turned in his chair to regard Harry with cold black eyes.

"Take a day to think this over." He leant down to pick up his brief case. "My employers want that priceless jade artefact back and they specifically requested your services to get it. Believe me when I say, no one walks away from them."

"Appreciate the warning, but I'll take my chances." Harry tipped his head toward the door. "Now get out."

Jones rose slowly and took a moment to straighten his suit. "You are making a big mistake today, Harry. Don't say I didn't warn you." With a tight smile he pointed to the photo lying on the desk. "Keep that for old times' sake. Compliments of my bosses."

The minute Jones was out the door Harry slammed it shut and turned to the photo.

He couldn't believe it. It was his Lou Lou. Older, of course. Black hair instead of silver blonde, but still her.

He began to pace. Ten steps to the window. What had she gone and got herself into? Four steps to the filing cabinet. Stealing a priceless piece of jade from some heavies? Ten back to the wall. And why did those creeps even know about Lou and him? He returned to the filing cabinet and gave his favourite spot a good kick. Tomorrow he'd start digging into Mr Jones and his tough guy bosses.

He stopped pacing and walked back to the desk. Picked up the photo and gazed into her eyes. His beautiful Lou Lou.

"Time to admit it, buddy." Harry closed his eyes and took a deep breath. "You've been kidding yourself all these years. You will never, ever, be over her. One lousy photo and it's as if the last ten years never happened."

He dropped into his chair with a sigh. "I wish you all the luck in the world, Lou. I think you'll be needing it." But what he needed now was whisky, and lots of it.

He'd just shrugged into his jacket when his phone pinged.

New client. At Rick's in ten minutes. Mrs Smith. Cheating husband.

Perfect. Two minutes walk to Rick's, another twenty to deal with Mrs Smith, and then he could concentrate on getting well and truly hammered. And forget Lou.

A few minutes later he stepped into Rick's Bar and its reassuring miasma of stale beer and cigarettes. Jake, the barman, tipped his head toward Harry's usual booth.

Excellent. Mrs Smith was waiting.

He wove his way through mostly empty tables to the back of the bar where things were even darker and quieter. When he reached his booth and his eyes hadn't yet adjusted to the low light, he could only see well enough to know Mrs Smith was sitting in his usual spot, facing the room. Annoyed, he slipped into the booth.

"Mrs Smith?"

"Hi, Harry."

Harry's heart missed a beat. He knew that voice. Gradually the figure sitting across from him came into clear focus. "Lou?"

"Yep."

She'd changed her look again. Brown hair cut short and choppy. Slim, but stronger looking than he remembered. The bright blue eyes he used to dream about now chocolate brown. But she hadn't changed her lips. They looked full and soft as ever.

She gave him a small smile. "Like your office."

"Yeah, well, some people are more comfortable talking in here."

She leaned forward and he caught a breath of her soft scent. Something expensive and French. Nothing like the light floral she used to wear.

"You look good, Harry."

"So do you. I ... " He was all at sea. Past and present were colliding, confusing him. This was his Lou. She was in trouble and she'd come to him. But if he stayed here he was risking his heart again. What to do? "Oh, Christ," he muttered. "How much more can go wrong in one day?"

"Harry!" Lou's eyes flicked over to the door, watching each new customer closely. "Concentrate. I need your help."

"For God's sake, Lou. Can you cut me a break? It's been ten long years since I saw you. After you left without a word." Anger grabbed at him, threatening to overwhelm. "Do you know how hard I tried to find you? How long I looked?" It was a struggle now not to yell. "You broke my heart, Lou."

"I know, Harry."

He watched as a single tear rolled down her cheek.

"And I'm so very sorry."

Harry felt all the anger drain out of him, leaving him empty. "Aw shit, Lou. What happened?"

"Please believe me when I say I thought I had no choice," she said.

"Not enough. I need to know why."

When she stayed silent he stood up. He'd had more than enough for one day. Whisky awaited. "Then it's goodbye, Lou."

"Harry." She looked him straight in the eyes and said, "Silver bullet."

Everything shifted in that moment. Pieces began to fall into place. "What did you say?" he said.

"Is there something wrong with your hearing these days?" she said with a grin. "I said silver bullet."

Harry sat back down. "You're a Central agent. I'm your local operative. Well that changes things." He leaned out of the both and waved to Jake. "Let's get a drink and tell me your situation."

"Okay" She rolled her shoulders and leaned back a little. "Coffee, please. Black. Two sugars."

After Jake left with their order Harry said, "So while we wait, fill me in."

"Like I said, I need your help." She ran her fingers through her hair.

Harry remembered she did that when she was tired.

"I know," he said. "My last client wanted me to find you. A Mr Jones, who said you were nothing but a cheap little thief who'd stolen some old jade thing. He did not take it well when I knocked back the case. Got quite nasty. Vague threats were made. I didn't like him and I'd really like to meet up with him again sometime.'

"The way this case is going, it's highly likely," she said before checking out the bar again. "Barman's coming back."

Jake slid the coffees onto the table and said, "By the way, some nasty looking dudes have been in here last few days asking after you. Showed me a pic of the lady, too. My boys are here. In case."

"Thanks man," he said to Jake's departing back.

Lou raised an eyebrow.

Harry smiled. "Jake's one of ours. His boys just love a fight."

"Good. Backup is good. We may need them."

"So what's the situation?" he asked.

"I was sent to steal the formula for a vaccine. It protects against a new biological weapon that has the potential to wipe out every unimmunised human on earth." She scanned the bar before putting a hard-sided case, around six centimetres square, on the table.

Harry picked it up and opened the cover. Inside was a piece of jade covered in what looked like ancient Asian decorative carving. He looked at Lou. "Really?"

"Yep. It really is an ancient artwork. Got to hand it to them, that's clever concealment. The formula is hidden in the carving. I came through customs as a courier taking it to the 'Jade Throughout the Ages' exhibition at the Art Centre."

Harry noticed she had dark circles under her eyes. "You look tired, Lou."

"I am. This has been a long solo assignment. I've got this far alone, but now I need help to dodge the guys who want the jade back."

"Okay." He went to hand it back. "What's the plan?"

She waved his hand away and leant forward. "No, you keep it. If things go pear shaped, they'll go for me. I don't need to tell you this is important, Harry. If I go down, you have to carry on and get it to Central."

Before Harry could protest she added. "And that's a direct order."

Harry slid the jade into his jacket pocket. "So you've been in the service for ten-plus years?"

She nodded.

"You must be pretty senior by now."

She nodded again. "Senior enough."

"I've been in five years," he said.

"I know," she said. "Word gets around who's doing a good job."

"Good to know," he said. "Well, that's the work portion done. Now tell me why you left."

"You're kidding, right?"

"Nope."

"Harry, we don't have time for this. Jones and his goons are on my tail."

Harry leant back and gazed at her. "I'm making time."

"Oh for God's sake, Harry." Her eyes bored into him. "Will you give it up? We need to get the jade to Central. My assignment is more important than us."

"Jake is out there. He'll warn us if they come. Now tell me."

"I could order you again."

"Really?"

With a sigh she slumped back into the seat. "Okay. I was recruited at uni. A perfect candidate. Asian studies. Fluent in three languages. No family, no commitments."

The 'no commitments' comment stung.

She picked up a coaster and started worrying at it.

"So you've told me why you disappeared," he said. "But not why you left me."

She started shredding the coaster. "You won't like my answer, Harry."

He didn't think he would either, but he had to do this, hear her out. Then he would seal up his heart again. Forever. "Tell me Lou. Please." He took a deep breath. "I've never gotten over you."

She threw the tattered coaster down and took his hand. "Okay. Truth."

Even after ten years, her touch was so familiar. The same warmth and care with a little buzz of electricity ... just like the old days.

Lou looked at their joined hands and murmured, "Just like before. Hasn't changed one bit."

She gave his hand a gentle squeeze and lifted her chin. "I

loved you, Harry. So much it scared me shitless. I was terrified we'd do all we planned, like my parents did. We'd start a life together, get jobs, a house, kids, and then just like them, one day we'd look across the table and realise we didn't know one another anymore. Strangers simply going through the motions of life. Our great love lost and us left ruined and broken."

She let his hand go and leant back. "I couldn't risk it. I just couldn't let that happen. What we had was too precious." She checked the door again. "I've always loved you, Harry. Still do. When I sit here and look at you my heart swells and I want to kiss you and lie in your arms and be safe forever."

"You love me?"

"Yes. Now, we've spent long enough on this. We have to go."

Harry was too confused to argue. She loved him ... yay. But she'd left him just in case?! He couldn't get his head around it. They needed to talk more, work through it. Surely there was hope. But she was right. This was not the time.

"Shit!" She closed her eyes for a moment. "I just realised something." Lou scanned the bar again before looking at him. "The fact that they came to you ... my cover is definitely blown and probably yours, too. That's the only way they could've known about us. And that means they expected me to come to you."

"Christ," said Harry. "You're right. We've got to move."

Lou began to slide out of the booth when Harry heard the bar door slam, followed by the sound of a shattering bottle. "Stop," he hissed. "That's Jake's sign. Trouble."

Lou peered around the corner of the booth. "Yep. They're here." Pulling back she looked at him. "I hope you have an escape plan, because we're not getting out that way."

Harry smiled, "Don't worry, Jake and the boys will delay them long enough." On cue they heard voices raised and the scrape of chairs being pushed back.

Lou made to leave.

"No," he said. "Wait a minute, the show is just starting."

As the sounds of a fight erupted, she gave him a questioning look.

"I told you, Jake's boys love any excuse." Harry turned around and peered out. "Yep, all chaos in there. Follow me."

Grasping her hand, he slipped down the back passage to the fire door.

"You know there will be more of them out there," she said, her eyes sparkling.

"I know,' he grinned. "You can't know how much I hope Mr Jones is with them."

"You go high and left and I'll go low and right. On three," she said with a reckless smile.

God, she was even more gorgeous than before. "You know, don't you, that this thing between us isn't over yet. Not by a long shot. And when we finish this job, you and I are going to sit down and work things out."

Stepping closer, she wound her arms around his neck and stretched up to kiss him with such tenderness and love Harry's heart swelled with love and hope for the first time in ten years.

"Love you," she murmured as she pulled away and put her hand on the door.

"One ... "

"Two ... "

"Three ... "

13

GODDESS GAMES

SUE-ELLEN PASHLEY

Sophie stood in the early morning light and sucked on the cut on the tip of her finger. She wondered, not for the first time, if the Goddess would really mind if she picked the herbs rather than cutting them with the special knife she was supposed to use. Her mentor had started to come to terms with it in the end.

"Sophie," she'd said, "I think you need to find your own Wiccan style. Some witches do. You have to find what works for you and the energy around you."

Sophie turned over her wrist, looking at the small tattoo she'd got when her mother had died four and a half years ago. The Jade or Green Goddess, deity of compassion, family and love. She hadn't been going to get the Goddess. She'd been going to get a tattoo of a cat, her mother's favourite animal, but the Goddess had ... spoken to her from a sketch on the wall of the tattoo shop, and Sophie figured maybe her mother was trying to tell her something. So there she was, in all her small jade glory, a permanent part of her and a reminder of her mum. She brushed her fingers over the tattoo.

"You don't mind, do you?"

Getting no answer to the contrary, Sophie slipped the small knife into the pocket of her shorts and finished picking the plants she needed by hand—rue, yarrow, valerian, cohosh, rosemary and a few different types of bark, laying them carefully in her basket. She loved this time of the morning, with the bees buzzing around her and the world waking up to a new day full of possibilities.

Finished, she took her full basket inside, the cool air of the house a stark contrast to the heat already building outside, and ran her hand through her hair, trying to bring it to some order. Not that it ever worked. Her hair tended to have a mind of its own, the curls springing up however they wanted no matter what she did.

The spell book was already open to the page she needed—old Merl next door had asked her for the tea to help with her arthritis, since it had worked so well last time. Sophie's finger followed the recipe down the page ... and past it to the next spell. A love potion. She wondered if she'd ever be brave enough to make it. Not for Merl, obviously. At 87, she'd been married to George for 63 years and always said he was the love of her life.

No, Sophie wondered if she'd ever be brave enough to make it for herself. It had been two years—two years and four months actually—since Kevin had left to 'find himself'. Whatever the hell that meant. He'd only made it as far as the next town, though, so maybe he'd been easier to find than what he'd thought.

But a love potion? Sophie didn't know if she wanted to find love that way. Someone compelled to want her—to want to be with her. No, she wasn't at that point. Not yet anyway.

The sound of the doorbell interrupted her thoughts and she frowned. Who could it be, this early in the morning? The front door stuck, as it always did, and she yanked it open, flakes of paint coming away as she did.

Holy mother of Goddess, the sight before her. He was ... beautiful. Brown hair flecked with gold in a way that looked natural, not salon made, a chiselled jawline with just the right amount of stubble, and blue, blue eyes framed by dark lashes. She wondered if she'd actually completed the love spell in her sleep.

CHRIST, he barely remembered why he was there. Like a thief, the sight of her literally took his breath away. That brown tangle of curly hair with ... was that rosemary in it? Brown eyes that reminded him of the toffee his grandmother used to make when he was a kid, and even though she only come up to his shoulders, curves that made him forget who he was for a second.

She frowned at him. "Can I help you?"

He had to consciously remember to swallow.

"Oh, yeah. Hi. I'm Michael."

It took a second for his brain to realise that that probably wasn't enough information. Jesus, talk about smooth. What was it about gorgeous women that made him unable to form complete sentences?

"I'm from—" He touched the name on his shirt.

"Michael's plumbing," she finished for him, frowning.

He had an insane urge to reach out with this thumb and gently smooth the line between her eyebrows. Thankfully his brain was working well enough that he was at least able to resist that.

"We had a call about a plumbing emergency."

She shook her head. "You must have the wrong address. I didn't call anyone."

"Are you sure?" He checked his phone. "Six Butterfield Road?"

She nodded. "Yes, that's me, but—"

Her words were interrupted by the sound of gushing water and he watched her eyes widen with surprise before she turned and started running. He raced after her, straight into the kitchen, where the tap had gone crazy, spraying water in every direction, soaking her as she tried to put her hands over it to stop the flow. Not that it was doing any good. In fact, it was probably making things worse. He came up beside her.

"Do you know where the mains are?"

She nodded.

"Go turn them off."

She fled and he looked around, trying to find something to wrap around the tap. A tea towel, a piece of cloth ... anything!

Nothing.

He sighed and unbuttoned his shirt, wrapping it around the tap, trying to contain the damage. It was only a few minutes before he felt the pressure stop and she came back inside.

She was soaked, and Jesus, everything in him clenched at the sight of her. God, what was wrong with him? He was 27, not 17!

HOLY MOTHER OF GODDESS, he'd taken his shirt off! She knew she was staring but she couldn't seem to stop herself. Brown, well-shaped shoulders that directed her attention down to arms that stopped just short of being too muscled. And abs ... *oh my* ... abs that rippled down to disappear into his shorts. Holy crap, she was staring at his crotch! Mortified, she managed to bring her gaze up to his face again. A face that was now a light tinge of red, which only made her want to touch him, just to see if his skin was warm. Dear Goddess, was it wrong to be wondering what a complete stranger tasted like? She thought it probably was.

"I'm so sorry," she said. She didn't know if she was apologising for the tap or for herself. She suspected the latter. "That was the weirdest thing. I wasn't having any problems with it before."

He gave her a quizzical look, one that made his blue eyes crinkle at the sides.

"That *is* weird."

She moved closer to him. "What do you think the problem is?"

"I'm not sure." He was breathing fast—well, faster than what she thought was normal—and she wondered what it would be like to put her hand on his bare chest, if she'd be able to feel his heartbeat...

She shook her head. That was just wrong. She needed to get a grip. He was a perfectly nice (very, very nice!) man here to do a job (that she hadn't known she'd needed), not to fulfil the needs of an obviously strung out, physically needy witch. Although it had been over two years.

Stop it, she told herself.

"Can I do anything to help?" There, that was better. Friendly, not needy. Or gropey.

He opened his mouth slightly, as if he was going to say something, but then shut it again and closed his eyes for a second, taking a deep breath. She found she was staring again and looked away quickly when he opened them. She felt like she was a teenager, staring at her school crush.

"I'll go and get my toolbox. You might want to," his hand flicked around the kitchen, "mop up a bit of the water before it damages anything."

"Mopping duty. Got you. Consider it done. Can do. Ten-four." What the hell was wrong with her? *For all things holy, shut up!*

She grabbed paper towel from the cupboard and started to mop up the puddles that seemed to be everywhere, patting a

damp strip against her face for a second in an effort to cool
herself down. She hadn't been this hot and bothered for a
long time. Probably for a long time before Kevin left if she was
honest. Not that he hadn't been cute, or that she hadn't
fancied him, just that, well, things had got... boring by the
end. Like neither of them could be bothered to try anymore.
In some ways it had been a relief when he'd said he was
leaving.

The sound of a clearing throat brought her back to reality
and she looked up at him from where she was kneeling on the
floor. He looked even better from that angle. He was just
standing there and she wondered if he felt the attraction as
much as she did. Maybe that's why he was silent, watching her.
Until she realised she was in front of the sink and he couldn't
get past. Dear Goddess, the humiliation!

HE DIDN'T KNOW where to look, what to do. Christ, she was
going to think he was some sort of psycho pervert rather than
the professional he was. The professional who'd been building
up his business for three years now, using the money his dad
had left him in his will. Wanting to do him proud. And now
here he was, acting like a hormonal teenage boy around the
girl of this dreams.

Girl of his dreams? Where did that come from?

He shook his head. *Get a grip, man. She's going to be
wondering what the hell is wrong with you.*

He moved forward towards the sink and put the toolbox on
the bench, trying to focus on what he needed to do rather than
her movements as she continued to mop up. It was hard. Really
hard. And then, suddenly, she was next to him. Close. Close
enough that he could smell her. Earthy, sweet ... delicious.

She was staring up at him, her lips—pink and soft—parted

as her eyes went to his arm. To the tattoo he'd got there three years ago, when his dad had died.

"The Jade Goddess." She whispered the words and his muscle quivered under her touch as she traced the lines with her fingertip. He forgot to breathe for a moment as he watched her, mesmerised by the feel of her touch on his skin.

"I wasn't going to get it," he said at last, "but she... I don't know... "

"Spoke to you," she finished for him, and all he could do was nod.

She turned over her hand, showing him his tattoo's smaller twin on her wrist, and he took a step back. Bloody hell! What was going on here? The phone call, the visit that wasn't needed until he was actually here, and now matching tattoos. With a woman he'd never met before.

"I don't understand. What does that mean?"

"The Goddess?"

"No. All of ... this."

"I don't know," she said. "Maybe it doesn't mean anything."

And even though that didn't feel right, he was happy to go with it. Because the alternative was downright scary, no matter how sexy she was, no matter how much his fingers wanted to get caught up in her hair, no matter how much he wanted to nuzzle into her neck, following the line of her collarbone with his lips...

Christ. *Stop it!*

He unwound his shirt from around the tap, and even though it was soaking wet, putting it on at least gave him some sense of dignity. Soggy dignity, but dignity all the same.

"Okay, well, I'll have a look at the tap then, shall I?"

She nodded, biting her bottom lip in a way that made his blood heat up to danger levels. Hot sun on the beach levels, where all you wanted to do was shed your clothes and leap into the water.

"Is there anything I can do?"

He tried a smile. "No, all good."

"I could dry your shirt for you."

"No!" Christ, that was way too fast; too loud. "I mean, it's okay."

"Okay."

SHE STOOD THERE, watching him, unsure what to do, even though this was her house. To be perfectly honest it was hard to look away, and part of her was happy to stand there and watch him pull the tap apart. Really, really happy. Happier than was probably socially acceptable.

She leant against the bench. "When did you get your Jade Goddess?"

His eyes flicked to her before looking back to what he was doing.

"Three years ago. After my dad died." She heard a small catch in his voice. The same one she still got when she talked about her mum. "What about you?"

She took a deep breath. "Four years ago. After my mum died."

His hands stopped moving for a moment, so she knew he'd heard, but he didn't look at her this time. She tried to ignore the small sliver of disappointment that lodged in her chest. She didn't even know his last name ... how could she be disappointed?

"I'm sorry. I didn't even ask your name." His voice was deep, and even though he still wasn't looking at her, her heart increased its tempo, like it was performing a solo tango.

"Sophie. Sophie Greenwood."

He did turn to her then, giving her a small smile that made her whole chest ache.

"Pleased to meet you, Sophie. I'm Michael *Black*wood."

She laughed then, and he laughed with her.

"So, Sophie Greenwood, what do you think is going on here?"

She shook her head. "I have absolutely no idea."

He nodded and then put his tools away before turning back to her. "There's nothing wrong with your tap."

HE WATCHED her eyes widen in disbelief and the faint feeling of being set up slipped away.

"What do you mean? It was spraying water everywhere!"

"I know. But it's in perfect working order. Doesn't even need a new washer. The only thing that could possibly, at a stretch, have caused it is a major change in the water pressure."

She cocked her head at him. "So what do you think? Should I turn the mains back on?"

It sounded almost like a dare and he nodded at her, trying not to let the nerves he was feeling show. God, she was gorgeous. And funny. And he wanted the tap to be fine when they turned it back on. He wanted this to mean something, even though that thought scared the hell out of him, too.

She nodded and went back outside. He waited, trying to get his breathing under control and it seemed like forever before she was back there at his side. She looked up at him and he could see the nervousness in her eyes as well. It made him feel better. Like they were in this together.

He flicked the lever of the tap and it came out in one even stream—perfectly well behaved. He couldn't stop the smile that came to his face or the balloon of happiness that seemed to be swelling in his chest.

She was smiling back at him. "Well, will you look at that."

And then, before he could change his mind—before his

rational brain told him to stop and think about the fact that he'd only just met this woman and don't do anything crazy— he moved closer to her. And without hesitation, she turned her face up to him. Her lips were soft, softer than he thought they would be, and her hand came around the back of his neck, pulling him closer. He cradled her head, his fingers tangling in her hair the way he'd been thinking about from the first time he'd seen her, while the other traced down her spine, pulling her closer to him. Her body moulded to his, fitting like she was always meant to be there. With him.

And all he could think was that he was home.

14

THE DRAGON PENDANT

DAVINA STONE

Every Saturday Mia walked past the young guy who ran the gem stall.

She came here each week to buy her fruit and vegetables because they were cheaper and fresher than the supermarket. She loved the busy vibe of the undercover markets, the smell of freshly brewed coffee, and the bratwurst and onions she only ever allowed herself once a month as a treat.

And so it just happened that she often found her eyes glancing in the direction of his stall.

He had an exotic look. His skin was the colour of a café latte and his eyes sparkled dark under a soft black fringe. He stood there and smiled at passersby, his bum bag slung loosely over his jeans, his arms a lovely play of muscular grace as he opened cabinets for shoppers, bringing out the little pieces of stone, the carved bangles and more sophisticated rings and pendants.

All in myriad shades of green.

Above the little stall there was a sign that read *The Jade Hut*, and next to it some Chinese hieroglyphics. Mia guessed they probably spelled the name of the stall too, but she really didn't know that for sure. She had no idea if the language was Cantonese or Mandarin.

Every week Mia paused, smoothing her unruly auburn curls into some semblance of order, willing herself to have the courage to go over. And every week she sighed and sidled past to buy her apples and oranges, her bunch of kale, and other green and healthy things.

But not today. Today Mia stopped and fingered the little piece of engraved stone in her pocket.

She hesitated then walked over. The guy, who had been re-arranging some pieces of jewellery in a glass cabinet, looked up and smiled straight at her.

"Hi," he said and Mia's heart did a strange little backflip. "Can I help you?"

Mia gripped the stone and felt how hard it was under her soft fingers.

"I was wondering if you could take a look at something for me?" she said quickly, before she could regret it. "I think it's jade but I'm not sure. Someone gave it to me."

She thought of Mrs Singh, how her old face would crinkle with a sweet smile, and Mia felt a lump in her throat, tears pooling behind her eyelids.

Don't cry, not here in front of the Jade Hut guy.

He looked at her kindly and she felt that those dark eyes could see right into her soul, laying bare all her secrets.

"A gift from someone special?" he asked softly.

Mia nodded mutely.

How could he tell that?

"Do you know anything about jade?" she asked to try and steer away from thoughts of Mrs Singh and the possibility of a meltdown in front of a stranger.

His lips twitched. He had a beautiful mouth. She found herself wondering what it would be like to kiss him, and felt a blush rising like sap.

"Yes, a little," he replied lightly.

Mia bit her lower lip. "Yeah, silly me," she said. " I mean, this *is* the Jade Hut. So I guess that's your job."

He grinned. "You're right to be suspicious though. So much of what gets called jade is fake."

"Is that what you sell? Fake stuff?" she said, disappointed.

He pointed with one slender finger to a tray at the front of his stall with bangles marked at ten dollars.

"They're fake. I don't pretend otherwise." He explained. "And these here are low quality. The pieces behind me in the cabinet are very high quality, originally from Myanmar. Expensive though. I don't get many sales."

"Is that good business practice?" Mia laughed, suddenly not so sad.

She liked the way his eyes held hers for just a little longer than they needed to. She liked the little fizz of her blood moving faster in her veins.

His grin was lopsided now. "Probably not," he said ruefully. "But sometimes beauty trumps business." His gaze still met hers more intensely than it should, so she had to look away, pretending to be interested in the contents of the cabinet just past his shoulder.

"Are you going to let me see it?" he asked after a moment.

Mia brought the carved dragon pendant out of her pocket. As he took it from her, their fingers brushed and she felt her breathing quicken at this miniscule touch of skin on skin.

What on earth was happening to her?

Was Mrs Singh's little piece of stone some form of alchemy?

He stared at it, and a small frown furrowed his brow.

He turned and picked up a small magnifying glass, placed the pendant and the eyeglass close to his face, and Mia let her gaze linger on the sleek ebony of his fringe falling forward as his neck bent. His fingers held the piece of jade like a caress.

He raised his head and she looked away, caught like a thief stealing pleasure at the sight of him.

"It's very—interesting," he said and his eyes burnt bright. "I have only ever seen one like this in a ... photo." He seemed to be thinking, as if trying to recall something important.

Mia licked her dry lips. "Is it real jade?"

"Oh yes, very real. I guess the question is how much is it worth? Are you wanting to sell?"

"No, oh no! Definitely not."

"Of course, I see. You said someone special gave it to you?"

Mia nodded. "Yes, an old lady I used to work with."

He raised a quizzical brow. "I thought it might have been your boyfriend."

Mia found herself blushing again. "Oh no, I don't have one," she said, thinking of Zach and how he'd left her, how he'd told her she was too sweet, too serious. Too boring for his trendy advertising exec lifestyle, he'd meant, but he'd stopped short of saying it. That was six months ago. It still hurt.

Did Jade Hut guy look a little pleased?

"Would you mind if I keep it overnight and check it out properly?" he asked.

She demurred, suddenly uncertain. "Um—I'm not sure."

"You know where to find me. I'm not going to do a runner. You come here every Saturday, don't you?"

Her eyes widened. "You know that?"

It was his turn to drop his gaze. "I've seen you pass by from time to time," he murmured then looked at her shyly. "I should introduce myself. I'm Ben. Ben Tan."

It sounded reassuring somehow, that name. Short and businesslike.

"I'm Mia. Mia Forsythe."

"Here." He grabbed a little velvet drawstring bag and popped the pendant into it. "I'll lock it in my cabinet and take it home tonight. I have extra equipment to check it for authenticity at home. Maybe we could meet tomorrow after I finish here. Would you be free maybe, um, for a quick drink?"

Mia stared at Ben. Her heart was doing a crazy little dance like a trapped bird against her ribs.

"Yes, OK. Yes, t--that would be fine. After work. Sure. W--what time do you close?" she stammered, feeling breathless.

"Sunday we finish at five," he said, looking pleased, then moved swiftly to the counter and picked up a business card and gave it to her. "These are my details and phone number. I promise your pendant is safe with me, Mia."

Mia put the card in her pocket where the pendant had been, then left to buy her fruit, her bunch of kale and other green and healthy things.

AT HOME that evening Mia tried to fill in her application for medical school. She had to keep saving the document on the computer because she couldn't get through the questions. She knew she wasn't stupid. She was just scared. Zach had always said that she wasn't scientific enough to study medicine.

For the last year, while she completed the bridging course in chemistry, she'd also worked part time as a care assistant at an aged care home near Fremantle. It started as a job and became a vocation, a labour of love. As she got to know each of the residents, they came out of the shadows and became real to her. Whether they suffered dementia or their bodies were twisted by arthritis and pain, it didn't matter to Mia. She loved the stories they told of their pasts, their old-fashioned jokes. She massaged their hands and brought them their food. She sat and she listened.

And that was how she got to know Mrs Singh in room eight.

Mrs Singh told her that eight was the Chinese number for good luck. She said she felt lucky meeting Mia.

Mrs Singh would sit in her chair, a tiny frail bird of a woman with bright black eyes like currants in a Christmas cake. She would tell Mia stories of Singapore in the 1950s.

"We so poor, so hungry then. Singapore very hard place to live. All changed now. People have food, homes, money," she would say in her still pidgin English, even though she had been in Perth since she was eighteen years old. She told Mia how her family had left Singapore in 1958, heading for Sydney, then her younger brother had got sick en route and they'd settled in Perth instead.

Mia asked if she had been happy here. And Mrs Singh had given her fragile shoulders a little shrug. "Happy, yes. But sometimes sad."

Mia had hesitated, not liking to ask why, because Mrs Singh's eyes had clouded over. Her mouth slackened as if she was lost in a memory that could not be shared.

One day Mia came in to find Mrs Singh in bed, looking even more frail than usual. But her lips spread into her sweet toothless grin when she saw Mia.

"Lovely girl. I have something for you."

She motioned with a bony finger towards her chest of drawers.

"Top drawer. Open please."

Mia did as she was bid. "Little red box. Bring it here." Mrs Singh said.

Mia gave it to Mrs Singh and watched the old lady's fingers struggle to open it, her hands shaking as she took out a small engraved piece of vivid green stone in the shape of a dragon.

"Jade. Very precious," said Mrs Singh, her eyes suddenly alive with emotion. "A special gift to me when I leave Singapore."

"Who from, Mrs Singh?" Mia asked.

Mrs Singh sighed; it was a rattle in her frail chest. "Man who love me. Man who I love, too. When I left he said he follow me. Join me in Sydney. But I never go to Sydney. I write letter to him, send it to Singapore. But no reply. I never see him again."

"Oh, Mrs Singh. That is so sad!" said Mia, feeling the tears prick her eyelids.

"It is OK," Mrs Singh said. "I met Mr Singh much later. Good man to me." She paused her eyes clouding, "But I never forget him. My first love." Then she brightened. "And now I give pendant to you."

"Me? Oh no, Mrs Singh. It looks too valuable. I could never—"

Mrs Singh was adamant. "I have no family, no children. You are my family now, Miss Mia. Dragon bring you very good luck. You take. Please."

Reluctantly, knowing how much this meant to Mrs Singh, Mia reached out and took the pendant carefully between her thumb and fingers. "Thank you," she said. "I will treasure it. Always. It's beautiful."

"Beautiful, yes. Like your green eyes, Miss Mia. Same, same. Jade pendant bring you friendship, too. Maybe even bring you love..." Mrs Singh lay back against her pillows and closed her eyes. She looked suddenly peaceful.

The next day Mia walked into Mrs Singh's room and found it empty, the bed neatly made up with fresh sheets. She ran into the corridor, a sense of panic overwhelming her. She met the agency nurse on duty. "Where is Mrs Singh?" She cried out, "Has she changed rooms?"

"Mrs Singh?" The nurse was measuring out pills into a little cup. "Mrs Singh? Oh yeah, little Chinese lady. Died in her sleep last night. Didn't they tell you at handover?"

Mia hadn't been to handover, she'd come in on her day off with Singapore orchids for Mrs Singh as a thank you for the dragon pendant.

Mia ran out of the nursing home, tears streaming down her cheeks.

MIA WAITED outside the markets at five minutes to five, her stomach a tight little knot of anticipation.

And then there he was at her side.

Ben. The Jade Hut guy.

"It's so nice to see you," he said, his smile finding its way into some deep secret place inside her. "I have good news for you, Mia. Let's find somewhere to sit."

They went to the busy Irish pub near the markets and sat outside in the late afternoon sun. Mia realised she felt happy for the first time in ages as Ben placed a glass of wine in front of her, then sat down opposite her and sipped his beer.

He took the pendant out of the little velvet bag.

"It's top quality, called Imperial Jade because of its luminosity. It's worth a fair bit of money, Mia. I've put it on a chain for you and I think you should wear it to keep it safe."

Mia thanked him as she fumbled to fasten the clasp around her neck and then asked, "How do you know all this stuff?"

"I'm a gemmologist. I did a diploma after my first degree," Ben said.

Mia felt embarrassed; she'd just thought of him as a stallholder. A *gorgeous* stallholder, but even so. "What was your first degree in?" she asked weakly.

"Chemistry." He grinned. "Guess you thought I was just an Asian bum migrant trying to earn a crust, eh?"

Mia blushed to the roots of her hair.

I thought you were the most beautiful guy I've ever seen, she thought, but didn't say it.

He looked at her face and just laughed. "I'm right, yeah?"

"No!" She said emphatically.

Ben shrugged. "I'm used to it," he said with the easy smile she was coming to love. "My dad's Singaporean, my mum's French. Makes for a strange combination in the looks department. Quite often people ask if I'm from South America. I enjoy them trying to guess my origins."

Then he changed the subject, his face suddenly intense. "Mia, I have to show you something important. Take a look at this."

He passed an old photo towards her across the table. It was black and white, faded, with curled edges. But Mia could still see that the delicately carved dragon in the image was identical to Mrs Singh's pendant.

Her jaw dropped. "Where did you find that?"

"In my grandfather's possessions," Ben said as he turned the photo over. There were words in Chinese on the back that she didn't understand, but Ben read them to her. "'Until we meet again. Gift to my beloved. 1958.'"

Mia's hand flew to her mouth. "Mrs Singh!" she whispered.

They stared at each other, both trying to understand what was happening.

It felt almost magical.

And then Mia explained everything to Ben: how Mrs Singh had left Singapore in 1958 to travel to Sydney, but had settled in Perth instead, and how she'd never found her loved one. Ben told her his grandfather had migrated to Sydney around the same time, and had remained single for many years but finally married his grandmother and they'd had one child, Ben's father. Ben had moved to Perth after his studies to live with his older brother, who worked here. Ben talked about his hopes and dreams to open his own upmarket jewellery business one day, importing rare gems—particularly jade.

Then he asked her about herself and listened intently as Mia poured out her own hopes and dreams of becoming a doctor, and how she struggled with chemistry.

"I could help you with the things you don't understand," Ben said shyly. "If you want, that is."

"I'd like that," Mia said, warmth spreading through her veins.

Later that evening Ben walked her to the station. As they stood on the platform he said, "It's such a weird coincidence. The pendant. As if it was meant somehow to bring us together. Sounds crazy, I know, but—" he paused and then rushed on, "Could I take you out, Mia? To dinner? You know, like on a proper date?"

They were facing each other and Ben's fingers lightly brushed hers, they were standing that close. So close Mia only had to move a tiny bit and their lips would touch. She closed her eyes and swayed into him, smelling the warmth of sandalwood on his skin and the sweetness of his breath.

And then Ben kissed her and she knew she had never been kissed like this before. His kiss was like drinking nectar out of a velvet cup. Her eyes opened, falling into the dark depths of his as reluctantly he pulled away and the train rattled into the station.

"Yes, Ben. I'd love to go on a proper date with you," she whispered huskily.

Then he wound his arms around her and held her close and Mia leant her head on his shoulder. She felt his heart beating against hers, and in between them, nestled safe as if it had finally found home, lay the dragon pendant.

SPICY BITES

Want to try something a little spicier?

Why not try our Spicy Bites Anthology?

SPICY BITES 2018:
CHAINS

Spicy Bites anthologies can be purchased from the Romance
Writers of Australia store http://romanceaustralia.com/shop/

LITTLE GEMS 2019

The gem for the 2019 Little Gems anthology will be...

TIGER'S EYE

For details of how to submit a story, please see Romance
Writers of Australia's website
http://romanceaustralia.com/contests/aspiring-contests/little-
gems/

Previous Little Gems anthologies can be purchased from the
Romance Writers of Australia store
http://romanceaustralia.com/shop/

ABOUT THE AUTHORS

Noelle Clark

Noelle Clark writes contemporary romance novels, rural romance, and historical fiction. Her books weave romance, intrigue and adventure into colourful and interesting settings. They feature characters who deal with love and loss; and who experience the often difficult facets of life such as forgiveness and redemption. Noelle lives in a secluded cottage in sunny Queensland surrounded by lush rainforest, and finds inspiration for her stories in the abundant nature around her and from extensive travel to exotic places. For more information go to www.noelleclark.net

Shayne Collier

Shayne Collier is a journalist by trade. Several of her short stories have made it into previous Little Gems anthologies (under the nom de plume Shayne Sands). She has at least three romance novels in "the drawer" and a completed 100,000-word ms targeted at the commercial women's fiction market that she plans to self-publish. Writing is her passion but she also loves ocean/open-water swimming, seeing live bands and hanging out with family and friends. You can follow Shayne's writing journey by visiting her website at shaynecollier.com.

Toni D'Alia

Toni D'Alia writes contemporary romance novels and children's stories. She worked as a teacher for a number of years, but made the change from teaching to writing and discovered her dream career.

Toni loves reading, going out for dinner, catching up with friends, movie nights and pyjama days. She lives in Victoria, Australia with her family who fill her life with love and laughter, and inspire and support her every day.

Isabella Hargreaves

Isabella Hargreaves writes Romance through the Ages. From the Anglo-Saxon and Danish frontier in tenth century England, to the English Civil Wars, to the Regency era and outback Australia in the 1920s, Isabella has a story to tell.

Her love of history surfaced in childhood. Now she works as a historian, researching and writing about people, places and events from the past.

Isabella lives in Brisbane, Australia with her family and a house full of pets. When she's not reading and writing, Isabella loves horse-riding and walking. She dreams of an around-the-world trip to indulge these passions.

For more information about Isabella Hargreaves see www.isabellahargreaves.com.

Sara Hartland

Sara Hartland is a hopeful romantic who wants all her characters to find their happy-ever-after. She lives on Queensland's beautiful Sunshine Coast which helps inspire her creativity and joy. Seeking the sunlight is possibly a natural response after a career in print journalism. It's much more fun writing about love and romance. This is her first short story and first appearance in Little Gems. Find her on Facebook and www.sarahartland.com to see what else she's been up to.

Dianne Inglis

Dianne Inglis has spent way too many years allowing work and all manner else get in the way of her true dream, to write. With her priorities refocused romance is at last flowing from her keyboard. This is her first effort at a short story, fitted amongst a plethora of novel ideas, her much longer, near completed manuscripts and a newfound energy for the writing future.

Jillian Jones

Jillian Jones is a writer and certified life coach residing on the beautiful Sunshine Coast, Queensland with her incredibly supportive husband, two creative children and a demanding Devon Rex cat. Along with affirming the deliciousness of hope, and how love transforms and heals, expect to encounter crystals, angels, clairvoyants, and the occasional portal when reading her contemporary romances. Her short stories feature in the Romance Writers of Australia Little Gems anthology,

2016, 2017 and 2018 editions. She holds a Bachelor of Arts from the University of Queensland majoring in English and Art History. Explore more at: www.jillianjones.com

Jeff Kenneally

This is the second venture into Little Gems for Jeff Kenneally having decided to extend his enjoyment of story telling into romance. A long running blog writer of human stories drawn from many years as a paramedic, www.facebook.com/Pre-Hospital-Practice-Hypothetically-Speaking or www.prehemt.com/category/an-ambos-life/, Jeff was once 'caught' sitting in the back of an ambulance reading a romance novel 'for research purposes'. Surviving that, he has moved into broader contemporary fiction writing.

Fiona Marsden

Fiona M Marsden started out as an avid reader. She was a late starter in finding romance novels, but once found, they became an addiction. Considering she wrote poetry and stories from a young age, it was only logical that the next step would be to write her own romances.

Published Work

"Medal Up" 2018

"The Runaway Christmas Elf," 2017

"Swept Away & Road Trip Baby" Li Family Duology, 2017

"Swept Away", Beautiful Disaster Anthology, 2016.

"The Sunstone Bride", "The Sunstone Inheritance", Little Gems Short Story Anthology 2016, RWAus.

"Heart of Stone", Little Gems Short Story Anthology 2017, RWAus.

www.fionamarsden.com

Helena Morrison

Helena has been a beginner writer for the longest time. So it's a good thing her writing group pals are not only very talented, but also very patient. She lives on the Mornington Peninsula with her husband and aside from reading and occasional attempts at writing, her interests include wine, food, travel, and playing golf quite badly.

Phillipa Nefri Clark

Phillipa Nefri Clark writes about life and love and mysteries, three of her favourite topics. She loves animals and nature of all kinds and is happiest on a secluded beach with family and friends. Her first books (River's End Romance series) can be found on all major e-retailers, selected bookstores, and her website. Phillipa loves hearing from her readers on Facebook, Twitter, and Bookbub.

Jane Newton

Jane Newton is an avid romance reader. She is also an editor who has had the privilege of helping many authors polish their fiction manuscripts. Occasionally she writes stories of her own. *Jaded* is her second published romantic fiction short story and she is very excited to be included in the 2018 Little Gems Anthology.

She is currently working on a full-length sweet romance, in between editing projects and wrangling two tween-age daughters, a husband and a Burmese cat. You can find her online at janenewton.com, where she hopes to add more details about her published writing in the future.

Sue-Ellen Pashley

Sue-Ellen is an international author with three published stories: Aquila, When Henry Met Gina and Streamer, with her children's picture book, The Jacket, to be released in 2019. From being an avid reader and writer as a child to studying literature at university, she's always loved the written word and where it can transport her.

In her 'other' life, Sue-Ellen is a social worker and lives in Central Queensland with her family and a menagerie of animals, including snakes, turtles and lizards. She's an eternal optimist who enjoys making things difficult for her protagonists but loves a happy ending.

Davina Stone

Davina Stone wrote and illustrated her first novel at the ripe age of twelve. She spent her early years reading romances and practising kissing techniques on the back of her hand while waiting for her prince to arrive.

Eventually he did, whisking her from England to Australia on his motorbike. After a varied career she now devotes herself to honing her romance writing skills. Davina resides on the beautiful West Australian coast surrounded by a large crazy family and her muse, a small black dog who helps her to concoct plots on their daily walks together. Website: davinastone.com

www.ingramcontent.com/pod-product-compliance
Lightning Source LLC
Chambersburg PA
CBHW030651110726
47901CB00002B/666